The Elevation to Divinity

From Mistress Lucrezia to Goddess Ira

An adventurous and spiritual BDSM history at its best. It really held me. In fact, obsessed me.

Goddess Ira and Osiris

AuthorHouse™ UK Ltd.
500 Avebury Boulevard
Central Milton Keynes, MK9 2BE
www.authorhouse.co.uk
Phone: 08001974150

© 2012 Goddess Ira and Osiris. All rights reserved.

No part of this book may be reproduced, stored in a retrieval system, or transmitted by any means without the written permission of the author.

Published by AuthorHouse 1/13/2012

ISBN: 978-1-4678-8061-9 (sc)
ISBN: 978-1-4678-8062-6 (hc)
ISBN: 978-1-4678-8063-3 (e)

The creation of this story would not have been possible without the help, support and participation of some people. We express our gratitude to these people.

Any people depicted in stock imagery provided by Thinkstock are models, and such images are being used for illustrative purposes only.
Certain stock imagery © Thinkstock.

This book is printed on acid-free paper.

Because of the dynamic nature of the Internet, any web addresses or links contained in this book may have changed since publication and may no longer be valid. The views expressed in this work are solely those of the author and do not necessarily reflect the views of the publisher, and the publisher hereby disclaims any responsibility for them.

Table of Contents

Preface ix
1 Goddess Ira. The elevation to divinity of Mistress Lucrezia. 1
2 Ownership and collaring of Osiris. 11
3 Dominance of Goddess Ira intensified and submission increased. 27
4 Dangerous Goddess Ira. 40
5 Extreme. The black rite 59
6 Sadistic Goddess Ira in Japan and Egypt. 93
7 Sophisticated Goddess Ira 130
About the Author 163

Preface

What has happened is important for all of us. I have witnessed the elevation of the Extreme, Dominant and Sadistic Mistress Lucrezia into Goddess Ira who saved the world. I Osiris as her private writer have recorded her quest in this holy mission's manuscript. I was the first of her chosen ones and have seen a lot of what has transpired. She molded me as her BDSM instrument. An instrument needed for her divine mission which brought Goddess Ira to Japan, Egypt and Mexico.

Where possible, I described in the manuscript our relationship as personal as possible. I attempted to do this as honestly and as thoroughly as I could. Our relationship describes much more than the interaction between Goddess Ira as Top and me as Bottom. It describes our mutual trust and the absolute control that Goddess Ira has over me. When appropriate, I have included in this manuscript the feelings, thoughts, doubts and despair of myself and, where needed, Goddess Ira shares her private thoughts upon some matters or has added comments. Her corrections of course determine what is finally written, as she always needs to have the last word…no doubt about that.

Although at first glance, when I saw Goddess Ira, a tsunami of love and admiration swept through me it was during our journey through time that my love for her deepened more and more. My admiration and love for Goddess Ira are now etched forever into my soul. She is the love of my life.

Goddess Ira and I have concluded some time ago an ownership agreement of indefinite duration. Some are aware of this. By signing this agreement or contract I became the property of Goddess Ira. One of the stipulations of the ownership agreement declared that I have to be completely honest and open about my thoughts and feelings. The contents of this manuscript reflect this provision. Periodically I had to report in detail to the Goddess about my thoughts, my feelings and the execution of my assignments. The content of these reports are also incorporated into this manuscript.

Ultimately my love for Goddess Ira knew no boundaries. I have become completely dependent on her and my ego was absorbed into her ego. I have become part of her. There was no humiliation I could not bear for her and no test went too far. Even if these test were extreme and bizarre. At a certain moment I was so intertwined with Goddess Ira that while I drove my car her pictures appeared as in a slide show on my dashboard. This gradual development and my new life experiences are also described in this manuscript.

We think that we choose but generally we choose out of all the possibilities that are displayed in front of us the same things the same experiences again and again. Our life is based on repetition. But major life-changing events teach us something we didn't know. Give us something we never had or create a possibility we have never seen before. My major life-changing event was meeting Goddess Ira. Like most of us I also was hesitant at the beginning but I am grateful that Goddess Ira has gently led me into the unknown. It is Goddess Ira who makes the choices for me now. She has changed me and has demolished all my old values and replaced them by her respectable and pure values. My indestructible bond with my Goddess has become so strong that we now sometimes can read each other thoughts. She has become my soul mate.

This historical document is divided into seven chapters. Each chapter highlights one of the seven special qualities of Goddess Ira. These special qualities are: Gorgeous, Original, Dangerous, Dominant, Extreme, Sadistic, Sophisticated. The first letter of each chapter refers to one of these qualities.

The first three chapters are about the vision of Goddess Ira and the consequences this has for me. The next three chapters are about the preparation and the collection of artifacts needed for the fulfillment of the divine mission of Goddess Ira and the reason for my submission. The final chapter which took place in Mexico is about how Goddess Ira saved the world with the help of the Maya foundation and the new Maya princess.

> Only a few prefer liberty – the majority seek
> nothing more than fair masters.
>
> Sallust, Histories

Intelligent plan and vision of Goddess Ira.

1 Goddess Ira. The elevation to divinity of Mistress Lucrezia.

Dear Goddess you have ordered me to record your divine mission. What you read below is a reproduction of what happened and what we thought and felt. I also include, more or less, the notes which I wrote to you.

In this chapter your elevation to divinity is described. It all started in Egypt. Based on historical sources an international archeological expedition was planned in Egypt. Since I am an archeologist who knows a lot about Egypt they had asked me to join them. The historical sources they used described an ancient temple complex from the period of the Old Kingdom (3rd millennium BCE). Enthusiastically our team started with the excavations in the lower Nile valley. However the months passed without any success and after endless studying the historical sources I became more and more convinced that we had to interpret them differently but my boss didn't agree with my opinion. Over time our disagreement increased and we had heated discussion. At a certain moment when my frustration reached its peak I walked into the sandy dessert and got lost, not able to find my way back to the base camp. The sun was shining merciless and I became thirsty. The thirst got rapidly worse until I eventually hallucinated and fainted. When I regained consciousness I found myself inside a sarcophagus, a coffin, and looked into the darkness. My first awareness was that of enormous thirst.

You told me that around the same time you had a vision. In your vision, you entered an Egyptian temple. Egyptian priestesses accompanied you, opening the holy bronze door for you. In your vision you saw yourself descending a very long stairway and entering a dark cave, in the middle of which, an open colorful painted sarcophagus stood.

In this complete, deathly darkness I notice two points, coming closer to me. I couldn't see the eyes and yet I knew that two eyes stared at me and that these two eyes belonged to a body. Slowly the silhouette of a beautiful slender woman with long hair became into view. She wore a black catsuit made of latex with thigh-high heeled black boots; the catsuit was high cut to her waist. This gorgeous woman had beautiful breasts. The boots were high heeled and reached up to her slender upper legs a crushing appearance that stimulated my fantasy. Love flowed through me like a tsunami. I felt that I was lost to this sophisticated woman and that I was forever hers. She took a jar which stood next to the sarcophagus. I could see the color of her hair and eyes. The hair was dark black and the eyes were magnificently green, hypnotizing me. I saw an elegant, dominant, dangerous and sadistic woman of the worst kind. I was aware of her presence, I felt her power and I shivered.

Behind me I heard a voice that spoke to us. Nevertheless I knew for sure that I was alone with her and that she wasn't the one who spoke. THE VOICE said "it is time to fulfill the prophecies. You will be the daughter of Maat and your divine cosmic goal will be revealed because only you possess the seven qualities by nature. Make the brandings and impress the sign of Maat first. After that your name will be revealed" The voice showed us brief glimpses of our future. I saw my body naked and defenseless while you were doing things to me. I saw how you heated up fire irons. I heard myself yelling and saw myself fighting against the cuffs and the ropes.

"You will be her instrument and anvil and be born again THE VOICE said. She will give you a new name. Seek the daughter of Maat, mentioned in the prophesies of the Maya, and drink her nectar. It will bring blessings. The papyrus scrolls shall show you the way. You are the messenger and the key to Goddess status". Then there was silence and I saw how the silhouette faded away while the jar fell to the floor. I was awake. I didn't dream anymore and saw that I lay in a sarcophagus painted with the picture of Osiris. It was easy to recognize the green skinned Osiris because he was depicted as a mummified pharaoh with a white atef crown with feathers on the side. I stepped out of the sarcophagus and stumbled over the broken jar out of which the papyrus scrolls had rolled. I took the scrolls with me and walked out of the cave. Suddenly I remembered how to reach the base camp. After my unexplained absence, I felt that I was being watched constantly.

As an archeologist I of course knew that Maat was an Egyptian Goddess and that she was the protector of the cosmic order. She symbolized the inevitable course of nature and was responsible for the cycles of life and represented the embodiment of the laws of our existence, truth, law and world order. Maat wears in her hair band the feather of truth.

Osiris is also an Egyptian God. Osiris was not only the god of kingship and vitality of the Pharaoh (the king of Egypt); he was also the personification of fertility. He was Lord of Hades. When the dead came to his throne, the heart was weighed by the feather of Maat. If the dead had led a life in conformance with the precepts of Goddess Maat, the heart was light and the person was welcomed into the afterlife. The weighing was done by Goddess Maat herself. If the heart was heavier than the feather, because of the sins committed, the heart of the dead person was eaten by a monster called the "Devourer".

I translated the longest script on one of the papyrus scrolls first. I didn't understand the script at first. On that scroll was written: Daughter of Maat found by seven words. Her name is hidden. Her divine circle is carved by fire. The name Goddess glows in darkness. Her cult is peace. She is the code. The living water fulfills the prophecies.

Suddenly I thought of the Mayan calendar. The Maya calendar is actually the remnant of a much older calendar system that dates back to the Big Bang which indicates the end of time. The end of time would take place according to certain scholars on December 21, 2012. That would be de day that the creator coincides with his creation. I knew that certain secret societies were preparing for this day. At that date they would grasp world domination. According to the prophecies of the Maya this could only be prevented by the daughter of Maat and her helper Osiris.

Dear Goddess, the translation of the other papyrus scrolls were not so problematic. It were seven words: Gorgeous, Original, Dangerous, Dominant, Extreme, Sadistic, Sophisticated. The command in the cave had been clear. With these seven words I could find the daughter of Maat. The right order was also obvious. If the first letters of the words were put in the right sequence, the word GODDESS arose. These words were my only link to you the gorgeous woman I had seen in the cave. I sought an extremely beautiful lady who possesses all the seven special characteristics. A woman whose silhouette I had seen. The search to find you had been quite a challenge and has taken a lot of time.

Dear Goddess, you have told me so often that coincidence doesn't exist. I believe you. Now I know you are right. The following proves e.g. that your are right. On a fetish festival an attendant gave me your business card. On that card was written "extreme in everything". The word "extreme" triggered me and I felt a strong urge to call you to make an appointment. When I saw you I recognized you immediately, you were the woman from my vision, the daughter of Maat. The pieces of the puzzle fell immediately into place when I looked into your indescribable beautiful green eyes and shuddered -- clearly I would be your anvil. But I also felt an incredible feeling of love flowing through me. We both remembered the fog that enveloped around us and THE VOICE. The same thing happened now but this time THE VOICE said "it is now time to become Goddess Ira. Mistress Lucrezia you know what to do "and the memories of the cave floated into your consciousness. You brewed a special drink and made me drink it. It tasted a bit bitter and after swallowing my first measure of elixir, I went off to empty my bladder and bowel, so that I should not soil myself during the first initiation.

You brought out the fire irons. You lightly touched my skin and instinctively I pulled away; nonetheless, the branding irons left a trail at the places where the marks would be put. Cold shivers ran down my back. You noticed this and I received a second elixir which tasted sweet from you and you told me that during the making of the brandings I would be strongly tied because movements would spoil your divine marks.

You disappeared and after some time you came to fetch me. You felt soft and had a nice fragrance around you. I remember that you wore your black latex cat suit and black high heeled booths which I had seen earlier in the cave. And again I was impressed by your crushing appearance. I saw your strong and slender legs your beautiful curved ass and exquisite breast. Words can't describe how I loved you when you led me, like a lamb stumbling into that dark room. Without the help and support of you I certainly would have fallen but I didn't care I was with you the woman whom I loved. I felt weak from the numbing effect of the elixirs. You brought me to a room were the walls were painted a beautiful shade of blue. In this room a table was pushed closely against the cold stone wall beside the table stood a gynaecological chair. Next to the table were seven decorated candles which gave a warm yellow glow. You helped me to climb the table and put me into a straitjacket and tied me with chains. All the time you were talking to me with your melodious female voice to make it easier for me. I enjoyed your specific body odor. My hips were tightly buckled with leather girth straps. My thighs were stretched to each side and also tightly buckled with leather girth straps. My balls and my penis were fixed to my right thigh. A cord around my ankles at the bottom of the table completed my restraint. I was completely restricted and my phallus and balls were forced upwards into exposed prominence. Flashes of what I had seen in the cave came to me and disappeared just as quickly.

I remember that you gave me a third dose of the elixir which tasted salty. I dreamed away and hardly noticed that you had left the room. When you came back I watched, entranced at the red-hot fire irons which you held in your hand. You tested the heat of the irons and when you were satisfied you hovered over me while your soft hair touched my skin and without any hesitation pressed the first iron in my flesh. A gush of hissing smoke burst forth as my moist skin quenched the heat from the iron. A loud scream of my agony from the bite of the hot metal shattered the room I felt an intense pain when you had printed the first mark high at the inner thigh where it touched my left ball. The mark was that of the feather the symbol of the Goddess Maat. After that you made two more brandings. The pain became even more intense. If you read these three marks, which in fact are hieroglyphs, the name of you my Goddess appears. At last you put the hieroglyphic mark of Goddess high on my outer left thigh while I kept on yelling and fighting, to no avail. Much later during our joint journey true life I understood that from that time on Goddess Ira was my truth and my law.

I, Mistress Lucrezia, had been looking forward to this moment for as long as I can remember, giving a permanent sign and an oh-so-intense one as a branding. From the moment I had my vision, the branding irons have been on my mind, wondering why they were left at my place and by whom and why did I suddenly come across them? I knew they meant something but I did not see the connection with myself, until I asked one of my friends in the UK to go through his very old books to find the meaning of the symbols.

He told me they were hieroglyphic letters and symbols and he told me that the symbol of the sitting woman had to be placed behind the other symbols to give it strength, the strength of a goddess and the other three symbols represented letters: the eagle stands for A, the eye stands for R and the feather for I. But when I saw Osiris for the first time I immediately thought of him as the branded one. I just knew he would be part of my life from that day on but I needed to make him suffer for it, it seemed. To make him suffer did not seem like a punishment to me but rather a sort of ritual to make him different than others, he needed to be unique …And mine! So it was clear to me how I had to place the symbols as I knew what they were standing for.

When I had strapped him down I felt overwhelmed by power and excitement and pride, pride about myself for being able to have found a person to brand this way but also proud of the one I choose to brand.

The irons were glowing so nicely orange in the flames and the flames turned a bit blue and I could not wait to place my first sign on his body. When I saw his naked skin ready for me I felt so many emotions at the same time that I started laughing out of joy. The sizzling sound and smell of the skin burning was something I would never forget ever. To have so much power in my hands, to make another person mine by this branding ritual was a very great fulfillment of all my fantasies and seemed to bring me to a higher spiritual level at the same time.

Not only was I branding a person in a sadistic manner but I was actually performing an ancient ritual on him that had something holy in it, why else would there have been a goddess as one of the symbols? And it had to be me as the other symbols were the letters of my birth name, so am I some kind of Goddess? Is this my promotion after being a mistress or dominatrix for such a long time?

I can catalog this action as one of my spiritual, sadistic "brain"gasms…..

Then you set me free and I was ordered to turn over face down on my stomach at the table. My buttocks were unmercifully constrained and bulging from the tight leather saddle straps. My muscles resisted when, on the backside at the place where the thighs and buttocks join, three more marks were placed. Every time I screamed loudly, sobbed uncontrollably and the stench was unbearable. I couldn't bear the pain any longer. I heard, before I lost my consciousness, THE VOICE say, "Mistress Lucrezia, you are now Goddess Ira. Your special qualities make your divine mission possible. The circle of brands is the sign of our eternal covenant which cannot be broken. Your divine name was hidden in your artistic name. The circle symbolizes the above (heaven) and the below (earth) and your divine mission. Execute your mission as Goddess Ira and use your special talents which are described by the seven words: Gorgeous, Original, Dangerous, Dominant, Extreme, Sadistic, Sophisticated. You have to change Osiris into your Egyptian soul. Your Egyptian soul has to die. Your divine mission will not be easy. But never doubt you are the chosen one, you are the daughter of Maat."

For a moment I thought Osiris was hallucinating as he kept on repeating the same lines, at first I did not pay attention as I worried a bit that he might have been delusional because of the pain or did I perhaps brand too deep? I was quite sure I had done it exactly right and I was careful... but then I heard him repeating my name so I started listening to the words. Was this my divine mission in life?

It all seemed acceptable to me because that's how I felt: Divine -- fulfillment of my fantasies but on a very high, almost holy level. The words he was saying all seemed to have some relevance towards myself. But it was clear to me that Osiris wasn't aware what he was saying as he had passed out. I thought I'd ask him when he comes round. Divine, it kept spinning in my head. Me? Divine? The crown upon my work is to be promoted to Divinity!!!

When I came round, you were Goddess Ira and you had turned me again on the table. I looked closely at my brands. The shallow grooves where the iron had burned and sunk its way into my skin were brown and shiny and the surrounding area red and blistered - an ugly, wicked sight, painfully delicate to the touch. The room smelled of burned flesh and I was still tied. With the brandings you had purified my body, mind and soul which were essential for evoking divine grace in me, your devotee. However you my beloved Goddess were not yet finished. You started tattooing in my crotch. Just above my phallus you tattooed the eye of Horus. I remember with pride that you put extra lipstick on your lips and gave me a kiss which embraced the tattooed eye of Horus.

Yes the branding ritual gave me a huge kick and I was sooo high and light in my head because of it that I did not want the feeling to end; so I decided to give you a kiss as a reward, printing my red lipstick on your pubic region... I knew that would make you feel very fortunate and happy, but my little devil inside was smiling because my kind gesture would soon turn into another ritual of pain and creativity.

Horus is also an Egyptian God and his eye symbolizes protection and virility for the followers of the Gods. You explained to me that your mouth represents the primordial mound from which the earth was created. The enclosed eye signifies that you Goddess Ira will protect me and will guard over my virility. It meant that from now on you would take care of my spiritual and bodily nourishment.

I took my tattoo machine and red ink and started tattooing the imprint of each line of my lips so that the kiss of the Goddess would be there forever.....it was very beautiful and I was pleased with my work .

I was very happy that I had received this gift from you my much beloved Goddess. Your mouth also signifies that you as Goddess Ira represent the new creative force of this world. Subsequently just above your lips, to the left and right, you tattooed in hieroglyphics a secret code. The secret code was enclosed by two cartouches. Still you were not finished. Just above and between the cartouches you tattooed a caduceus which symbolizes unity and is achieved by the reconciliation of opposites. The snakes of the caduceus are the contradictory principles which play a role in the universe. Contradictory principles like woman-man, Top- Bottom, Dominant-submissive, Owner-property. The staff itself is the axis between heaven and earth, above and below. The wings stand for transcendence and divine trinity. I know that somewhere in the future Goddess Ira will explain the specific purpose of the staff.

I knew Osiris was proud but in pain, but the proudness was a much stronger emotion so he could not think about the pain now. I was sure he would be in pain for at least a week after these "artworks"... mission accomplished (with a smile)

Why one action led to another I can't really say, it was all like it was being handed to me by a higher force. Still bedazzled from the words of Divinity it all seemed to make perfect sense and all my actions were fluid, without hesitation and I just had to do it, this was my higher mission. I felt as if I had been chosen to be unique and I have always known I was different from others and life had put me in front of more challenges than any other person I know. Was all of that a test to measure my strength, physical, emotional and spiritual?

You had in the past, guided by divine hand, chosen the spider as your symbol. This symbol symbolizes your infinite creative power. Goddess Ira, who as a "spider" in its web, weaves the destiny of her chosen.

The first initiation for the chosen ones is the spider initiation. You then recited the spider incantation for me.

I, Goddess Ira, am your "spider",

I, Goddess Ira, carry in my web your creation,

I, Goddess Ira, weave your webs of delight,

I, Goddess Ira, give my chosen the right to exist,

I, Goddess Ira, grant the "spider" only to those chosen,

I, Goddess Ira, shall complete my divine mission with my little "spiders".

After a few days, the abused surroundings of the brands dried and flaked off, leaving clear imprints. Likewise, the tattoos healed perfectly. You had been graceful to me and I had been generous to you.

I understood that Osiris had to change his identity. But I didn't know what an "Egyptian soul" was. I asked Osiris. He told me that the Egyptians believed that the human soul was made up of five parts: the Ren, the Ba, the Ka, the Sheut and the Ib.

A part of the soul is a person's "name" (Ren). I had branded my name on Osiris so this part of my soul was by the branding incorporated in him. By branding my name he was forever connected to me. The Ba is everything that makes an individual unique. The Ka was the Egyptian concept of spiritual essence. The Sheut or shadow of a person was always there. It contained his personality. The Ib or metaphysical heart was believed to be formed from one drop of blood from the mother. To ancient Egyptians it was the heart and not the brain that was the seat of emotion, thought, will and intention. It was clear that Osiris had to lose his own soul and to assimilate my soul.

My vision and mission was to save the world. That meant also creating my "Egyptian soul". But I knew quite well that Osiris beliefs and perspectives shaded his expectations. He had his own lens through which he viewed the world. Through new experiences Osiris lenses had to disappear. It mend an immense shift away from his old ingrained habits and expectations. For this change in personality Osiris had to step out of his comfort zone. My lenses must become his lenses. He must, without any doubt, believe in my purpose. He must share my values, desires and interests. He had to identify himself completely with what I see, hear, smell and feel.

This vision of our future gradually developed in my mind and I began to develop a plan to get there. I started with a personal mission statement ("I am Goddess Ira who saves the world and Osiris will be my Egyptian soul") and I constructed in my kitchen a vision board. My plan consisted out of seven steps. Five steps were directed to destroying Osiris identity and two were building up my identity (my Ba, Ka, and Sheut) within Osiris. The first step (Ren) had been the branding of my name.

I never forgot my mission during the process of transformation of Osiris and was emotionally connected to my vision. I followed through with discipline and self-control. Each time I walked into my kitchen I saw the vision board with my mission statement and plan. When I had a spare moment I envisioned the absorption of Osiris into my body. The more detail I included in my vision the more clear my vision became. It was a continuous process of contemplation. The more I reflected on my vision, the more the pieces began to fall into place. My vision represented a formidable challenge and was unprecedented. Only a true Goddess can bring this vision to a successful conclusion.

2 Ownership and collaring of Osiris.

The household of Goddess Ira consists of the Goddesses certified by her and of submissive chosen ones. Goddess Ira can grant other Dominatrix's the Goddess certificate if they successfully have passed the prescribed course. But be warned, the methods of Goddess Ira are very original.

After becoming a "little spider" the Goddess decides whether you qualify for higher degrees of initiation. You then have to pass relevant (mainly) BDSM tests tailored to the personality of you, as the applicant. After the various initiation stages have been passed, Goddess Ira decides if the applicant will be collared and what will be his task in her household. It is very rare that a collaring takes place as Goddess Ira is very proud of her house and her life and lifestyle and she will not have anything or anybody take that away from her or damage that feeling

The applicants, the initially submitted chosen ones have to be tested and medically approved. Some of them will be transformed into latex dolls others will have to be submitted to torture or endurance or humiliation or medical experiments. It is clear that only those who successfully pass the heavy examination will prove to be useful to Goddess Ira.

I can imagine that you want to know what Goddess Ira requires in her tests. For example, she tests her chosen ones with the following practices

- *Bondage Domination Sado Masochism: Cock Ball Torture, Corporal Punishment, Bondage, humiliation, all sorts of training (horse, dog, maid, sissy, slut, service, toilet, furniture) and behavioral adjustments, complete re-education*

- *Medical play: enemas, sounds, catheter, anal stretching, needle play, sewing (suturing), tattooing, piercing, cupping, vacuum suction, pussy pumping, penis pumping, ball inflation and all her wicked, creative mind comes up with...*
- *Rubber Play: vacuum cube, triangle and bed, vacuum toys, rubber bondage bags, inflatable hoods and bags, rubber hoods and masks, rubber outfits, strait-jackets, rubber restraints, rubber prison, bungee suspension and rubber suspension and rubber trannies and rubber dolls*

In this chapter I wrote down my tests and my subsequent collaring.

When we met again, you took me to an exhibition about bees. There I saw incredible beautiful pictures of you. In one of the pictures you were beautifully dressed in a latex outfit. You were wearing a queen bee outfit. Your body and your beautiful curves were barely disguised in the transparent latex outfit. The latex dress had like the bees yellow stripes. And because it was transparent, part of your beautiful body was unveiled. You asked me, "Do you know why I choose this outfit?" I had no clue. You said, "I choose this outfit because the queen bee is the most exalted animal in wildlife. She is of particular importance because she represents eternal principles and notifies us when there is real danger. The queen bee symbolizes me. When I bring you into trance you will understand." You showed me another picture. On this picture you were wearing a black queen bee mask and you had a mischievous face. You said "mankind is just like bees, only a few can be queens and only a few are drone bees. What you will be is hidden in the stars."

In one of your performances as an artist you had performed and pictured the life of the queen bee. You, as queen bee, attracted the males with her pheromones however, the queen tried to escape the males, allowing only the fastest and the fittest males to mate. The mating took place during the nuptial flight and the males which did mate in your bride's flight fell dead out of the sky. Visually the nuptial flight was portrayed in a photo of you which I saw at the exhibition. My queen bee was lying on a bed supported by several hundred penises in the sky an astonishing view.

Then you took me to your hive and you said to me "to be suitable for the position I've in mind for you, it isn't enough that I extensively test you physically; it is also important that you continue your spiritual teaching. They are part of your Ka your spiritual essence. Lie on the bed with the 100 pricks and I will bring you to another world." As I lay down you lit the candles and the incense sticks. I had to wait and when you came back you had a short white short and a little black sweater on. I enjoyed how you looked.

You began with your magnificent voice your incantations and held a kind of incense stick to my nose which smelled like frankincense. Almost immediately I fell into a deep trance. I was in an ancient Egyptian temple and saw myself kneeling before you as you spoke to me. You were dressed as an ancient Egyptian Goddess. You had a narrow skirt on and wore a neck collar, bracelets and ear-rings. You had rimmed your eyes with charcoal, henna reddened your lips. And your finger and toe nails were varnished red. While I was kneeling you put both your elegant hands on my head. Bees were buzzing around you. You did not move your beautiful red lips nevertheless ancient wisdom entered through your hands into my brain and I learned:

- Spirituality is the recognition of the law of Karma and thus the fundamental unity of everything. We are all one. We have to learn how we can serve the universe and others.
- Coincidence doesn't exist in the universe. Whoever appears on your stage has a message or a lesson for you.
- You attract people and experiences to you as a magnet that exactly matches your unconscious needs, desires, doubts and fears. Sometimes our souls wait for a very long time for the arrival of these special messengers.
- The ego wants to remain the ruler. It wants to control, to hold and be acknowledged. The will and the ego must give way to acceptance and surrender.
- Spirituality is not about what your feelings or thoughts control. It is about accepting without protest the reality in your world.
- Spirituality, like love, is indivisible. Because you live in love or you do not.
- You can't make destructive, negative choices and at the same time expect constructive, positive outcomes.
- Not only with your actions, but also with your thoughts, feelings and beliefs, do you create.
- Spirituality changes your perspective on things and creates space in your experience. It has to do with surrender, letting go of concepts and ideas about how you should be, how you should live. It is learning to love reality.

- Meditation is not thinking, but being. It is to focus on the present moment and be where your body is.
- Words mean nothing without experience because they have no resonance in us.
- Spiritual knowledge is to dare see and to experience. And experience is not learning. Experience is defying our greatest human fear: life itself and to be fully human.

You ordered me to bring the learned principles into practice and to teach them to others. Since my unexplained absence in Egypt, I was being watched. I passed on your teachings to others. They must have noticed my change in behavior. They started to follow me more intensive. I do not know exactly when but at a certain moment they must have been convinced that you were the daughter of Maat mentioned in the Maya legend.

When I visited you Goddess Ira again I stayed overnight at your place. I tremendously enjoyed being with you. I noticed during this stay how intelligent you are and how much you know about art. How I loved to listen to your silver tongue when you spoke about all those things.

Art has always been a life-style to me … it's a drug and just like science I need to feed my brain with it … its pure luxury and a gift of nature to be able to create and to be able to enjoy the creation of others … I have spent most of my life philosophizing, learning or creating and it has made me who I am today ….

During this extended stay I was bound and whipped. You used enemas and put a steel tube in my urethra. You also liked to watch when I struggled in the bungee suspension. You fixed clothespins to my nipples and prick and when you moved the bungee suspension I felt a lot of pain. You had fun and often conjured a big smile on your handsome face. When it was night you chained me with my hands and feet to the floor and put me into an iron chastity belt. The whole night my prick was swollen and facing my feet. The next day you put needles through my phallus because it was inflated and started an extensive cock and ball torture. My balls were stretched by iron rings. You promised me that stretching my balls would continue in the future. I know now that you honor your word. With a very thick needle you pierced my nipples and with the same needle you made an Albert piercing through my penis. It did hurt but after a while I got used to it but I doubted if I was made of the material that you needed for your divine mission.

Before sending me home, you brought me into a deep trance/ hypnosis. I received the instruction that if you used the secret code I had to fulfill your assignments unconditionally. The first few weeks I had to listen daily to the recorded sessions and to repeat the given code mentally and visually four times a day. Each session should be at least a quarter of an hour and I also had to do daily exercises so that my body was in shape when I faced you again.

I knew that this was the moment to make Osiris feel who is in charge and to submit him to me in a way that showed respect towards him but kind of degraded him to become a dependant human being. I knew that after these rituals he would become addicted to me, but to the real ME, the whole person, in and outside, he would honor me, obey me, worship me, never doubt me, be supportive and he would never let me down. I knew that the pain I was inflicting, which made me smile as I am a natural born sadist, would be taken with pride and would have exactly the effect I wanted it to have, submitting to his Goddess. That's what I was going to be from now on, his Goddess, and a few wicked thoughts entered my head. I knew a few more "tricks" to keep him under my spell, but for now, he was so well under that I did not need any of my tricks to find him in the right kind of subspace, my divinely created subspace. All is divine, all has become divine and it feels like that on all levels. My divine mission to be a Goddess, to guide Osiris and perhaps others as well, towards the light. I was sure about my purpose in life and I kept being inspired by thoughts that were not present in my head before I had entered a state of divinity and Osiris was part of it, he would have to make notes or keep record, help me solve the puzzle. He would be my notary my private writer.

Was this the right time now, whilst he is in that subspace, to make him aware of the higher purpose of all of this?

I decided I would not tell him just yet but I would continue my rituals to make him completely dependent, I would not leave things to chance and decided I would need a few weeks to get him exactly where he needed to be. And for my own pleasure at the same time.

Another time you decided to make a semi permanent chastity belt. You did pierce countless times my penis and the surrounding area. My underwear was soaked with blood. After some time the pain faded away. I had to wear the chastity belt one week and when I had to pee in those days's I could do it only sitting. That was pretty difficult and embarrassing.

I could see that Osiris was having some trouble with what he had been through so I explained:" Embarrassment is also part of becoming a pure, unconditional, owned submissive to serve me without hesitation, embarrassment will clean the soul, and shame is something that will be

Goddess Ira and Osiris

part of your past. Shame and jealousy are two vices my owned one can't have and of course my wickedness enjoys the ritual in getting them out of your system"

We made a new appointment for further testing. As always I enjoyed your beautiful green eyes and girlish smile. You told me to undress and shower. Next I had to sit on the gynaecological chair and you put a tube into my anus so that I would be cleaned from the inside. When I was ready, I had to lie on the stretcher and you put pumps around my nipples. In my nipples were the piercings that you had put in at an earlier date. A Steel tube was placed in my urethra. Through the Prince Albert piercing a screw was turned. It did hurt a little because the screw was larger than the piercing hole. A little bit of my skin was turned around the screw. The screw was attached to the steel tube. Then you my beloved Goddess put a pump around my phallus. The pumps started to work and thanks to the pumps I got breasts. I think I was suddenly in the possession of at least a cup B a weird experience for a man. Also my penis became longer and thicker. You said that the penis pump would make my phallus stronger and you started to play with electricity. I clearly felt the current in my sphincter and in my genitals. When the electricity increased I could no longer take it and I felt relieved when you stopped.

I knew I could break Osiris very quickly with electricity as his body reacts against it as if he tries to protect himself from damage and of course I can't let him protect himself from Me? His body is all mine and he will learn to give himself, I have made up my mind that he will have to and he will, I am sure...his fear for electro play was just too easy to NOT take advantage of.....

You my beloved Goddess knew my deeply felt desire to love and serve you. You said "your wish shall be granted under certain conditions." We discussed the most important conditions. The main conditions were that I should give up my freedom and that I had unconditionally to obey you. My ego had to go. I would die and be born again. I agreed. However a last final ordeal I had to undergo. It would be very painful. You said in 15 minutes I will be back and you will know the treatment you have to undergo. You tied my hands above my head. Even my feet and my hips were tied. I was in an uncomfortable position. The time passed slowly. And then you suddenly appeared. In your hand you held a huge red-hot branding iron. It was at least 15 cm long on the branding iron were the letters Goddess. Part of me wanted to run away. You asked "are you sure?" I said "yes this is my ultimate act of sacrifice and commitment to you Goddess Ira." Slowly you pressed the immense red-hot branding iron in my flesh and again a gush of hissing smoke burst forth as my moist skin quenched the heat from the iron. The steam rose up. A loud scream of agony from the searing bite of the hot metal shattered the room. I smelled the smell of burnt flesh. It smelled awful, I smelled awful.

The brand was created at the front precisely at the boundaries of the abdomen and the thighs of my right leg. You told me "I know you cannot endure more now. But this brand will also be put on the backside if it heals well. If not I will put the four marks used earlier at a special occasion. The marks at your right leg will look like those on your left side like a garter. This garter is permanent just as your collaring and ordination will be permanent. I will send you the contract so that you have time enough to think it over. And if you haven't changed your mind you will be collared and ordained on your next visit to me."

The collaring would be my second major step in destroying Osiris identity. He would be owned by me. I thought about the contradictory principles of the snakes of the caduceus which I had tattooed on the pubic of Osiris. Soon very soon Osiris will be forever My property.

After the session we went for a lunch. Most restaurants were closed. But we found a cosy spot. You ordered for both of us champagne. Then we ate and drank deliciously. You also had ordered red wine which I liked very much. During our lunch we talked about anything and everything. Our conversation was lively. My heart glowed. It resembled a volcano which was on the brink of a gushing eruption. Unfortunately our lunch came to an end. I brought you back to your home. A few times I was so daring that I touched lightly your hand. I got into the car and drove away. But my thoughts and feeling hadn't left.

The next day I received the contract through the mail. I read the agreement and agreed fully with the content. I immediately let you know. A date was set for the collaring and ordination ceremony.

In the meantime I was instructed to use the secret code. By using this code I would fall into trance and go back to the ancient temple. There I had to prepare myself and to remember all that I had learned.

During the weeks that followed the brand slowly healed. The healing process was painful. Every movement felt like walking on nails. If a dust particle fell on the wound I almost had to cry. I wore during one month no underwear to diminish the pain. The pain was also joyful. With each painful move I thought of you my Goddess. I had been assigned to wear the steel pin in my urethra. Every time when I thought about you my penis swelled I felt also the uncomfortable feeling caused by the screw through the Prince Albert hole that did not move. Even now, as I am writing this manuscript, I wear the steel pin.

A new phase in my life had started. I pondered and prepared myself for my collaring and ordination. I knew that my Goddess is my life a life with her that I prefer over any other life. That knowledge determined the level of my being. My mind was clear. I was not concerned any longer with outer forms and conventions. I thought about you my Goddess and your creative power. In my connectedness with you Goddess Ira I endure in all eternity the perfect freedom. It is you who soon would make my choices. I felt for you Goddess Ira a love so profound that I felt completely fused with you. My love for you is serving and giving, not a love of taking or owning. It is not so much a physical manifestation as more a consciousness of the divine unity with you.

I could hardly wait for the special day. I was conscious of every thought and everything you had taught me. The day finally had arrived. I got into the car and drove to you. My heart was beating faster and faster. I pressed the door bell. The door was opened by you Goddess Ira. You said "before we can start the collaring sermon you have to be physically, mentally and spiritually clean." You brought me upstairs. When I climbed the stairs I saw the flag of you Goddess Ira hanging on the wall. You my Goddess ordered me to take a shower. I took a nice hot shower. Then I was ordered to take place on the gynaecological chair and to put my feet in the stirrups. You placed a tube in my anus. Fluid filled my intestines. Afterwards I had to go to the toilet and to empty my bladder. Physically I was then clean.

You commanded me to dress for the ceremony and when I was ready I had to call for the witness. I put on a tuxedo and a cummerbund and when I looked in the mirror I saw a sophisticated man. I was almost ready. I called for the lovely witness Charlotte and she attached the bow of my tuxedo around my neck. I was ready. The witness had dressed beautifully for the occasion. She wore a colorful dress that reminded me of Olivia Newton-John of the movie Grease. Her face and skin was strikingly thoroughly lily white. In her raven black hair she wore a white flower. She looked almost transparent and had a dreamy innocent look in her brown eyes. She asked me to wait in a room. While I was waiting I meditated about the ordination and collaring. I meditated on the bed with the 100 pricks.

Shortly afterwards she came to fetch me. I entered the hall and I saw the jewel and my poem which I had made for you Goddess Ira hanging on the wall. I carried a leash and a bouquet of forty-three red roses and one white rose to present to you Goddess Ira as a token of my enduring love for you, I felt completely devoted and full of trust. Charlotte was in the possession of the collar and the drafted copy of the agreement. In this agreement our obligations and responsibilities were stated. Charlotte knocked on the door and I heard clearly the strong dominant voice of you Goddess Ira say Enter.

The room which I had left was now semi dark. Candles and aroma sticks were lit. I saw several Egyptian statues. Then I saw you Goddess Ira. You looked gorgeous. You wore a three-toned latex dress. The collars of this dress were black, white and red. On the shoulders were silver spikes. This dress ended just above your knees and the shape of your good looking breasts was visible. You also wore black gloves. Your beautiful black hair framed your strong face. On your eyebrows you had used a black eyebrow pencil. You had also used black eyeliner and a little mascara. I had never seen such beautiful eyes before in my life. Your shapely legs were a feast for my eyes. You wore high heels and your toe nails were painted dark blue. You were gorgeous, sophisticated and seductive but also embodied a "devil". But what could I expect of a Goddess who is described with the seven words: Gorgeous, Original, Dangerous, Dominant, Extreme, Sadistic, and Sophisticated? Would you, my Goddess also be my "devil"? My heart burned for this "devil".

You carried a crop or dressage whip as a symbol of your dominance. You declared that Charlotte would act as witness of the ceremony. You said "that our witness belonged to the elected because she possesses from birth the positive and negative qualities needed for the achievement of the lofty status of Goddess."Of course Osiris did not know that the witness inherited these qualities... I would not tell him yet.....

A bell was rung by Charlotte to signal the beginning of the ceremony. I with leash and bouquet in hand walked toward you and offered you the bouquet and the leash. I said: "I offer the bouquet as a sign of my deep affection for you my Goddess. I offer this leash to you my Goddess so that you can guide me and lead me along my journey though life. I expressed my desire to belong to you and to follow you where ever you choose to take me."

You took the bouquet and leash from me and stated your acceptance of me. You expressed: "I accept your bouquet as a sign of your enduring love. I accept this leash as a symbol of the offering of yourself and give my promise carefully to guide you and lead you safely in my footsteps. You will belong to me from this day on and I will do all within my power to protect you as you join me on my journey."

You then asked me to kneel before you while you took the collar from our witness. You said: "will you kneel at my feet and take this symbol of ownership to wear as a sign to us and those we meet on our journey? With the placing of this collar around your neck and your acceptance thereof, I vow to do everything I can to be worthy of you. I promise to hold you and keep you safe, to honor you and to be sensitive to your needs. I acknowledge the trust you have placed in me and the responsibility that goes with the acceptance of that thrust. I will never violate or even threaten to violate that trust. I will always be open and honest with you. I shall accept the depths of your passion, devotion and trust and provide a haven where you are safe to express all desires to me. I will cherish our friendship. I acknowledge and accept with all my heart the gift of ownership you have made to me. Do you accept this symbol in the spirit by which it is given you?"

While kneeling I held my head straight but my eyes were looking to the floor. I proclaimed: "I kneel as a sign of my submission to you and acceptance of the symbol of your ownership. The collar you offered me is a powerful reminder of the control I have surrendered to you. I will wear it proudly for all of my days, Goddess Ira. With the collar I express the finality of my commitment to you and surrender my body, mind and soul to you. It allows me to do your will and allows me to follow in all directions possible. The collar is a solid symbol of my trust in you without fear of outcome and allows me to give myself to you. It is my desire to please and love you. The collar keeps me safely within your bond and excludes all other's powers over me. I agree to honor our relationship above all others, and seek to fulfill your needs and desires as you allow. I promise always to communicate openly and honestly with you keeping nothing from you. I promise to love, honor, respect and obey you for the rest of eternity.'

The witness then read the contract.

Ownership Agreement

Parties
......further mentioned as Goddess Ira;
And
....., further mentioned as Osiris.

Whereas:
- Osiris loves Goddess Ira as he loves nobody else;

- Osiris wants to express this deep emotion by signing this agreement;
- Goddess Ira has acceded this request and by signing this document the collaring ceremony is completed;
- the parties in full consciousness and in complete freedom enter this agreement;
- virtue, honor and integrity are an essential part of our relationship;
- this relationship is based on open and honest communication;
- this relationship is not based on physical punishment or restriction of privileges.

Agreed as follows:

Article 1: Ownership
By signing this deed Osiris becomes the property of Goddess Ira. The basis of this agreement is that the parties shall act towards each other with integrity, discretion and with much mutual respect towards each other. Osiris shall, besides the afore-mentioned basic principle, show his love for Goddess Ira through what he does and does not do

Article 2: Duration of this Agreement
This agreement is of indefinite duration and can only by mutual consent be modified or terminated. This agreement, like love, is of a perpetual duration.

Article 3: Obligations Osiris and rights of Goddess Ira
a. *Osiris shall obey the commands and assignments given by Goddess Ira. Although Osiris is allowed to make objections he may not refuse the given commands or assignments. Goddess Ira shall in her decisions take into account the objections made by Osiris.*
b. *Osiris shall do everything, without reservation, that is in his power to serve and please Goddess Ira.*
c. *Osiris hands his body, mind and soul unconditionally over to Goddess Ira. Goddess Ira accepts unconditional and unrestricted this disposition over his body, his mind and his soul. Goddess Ira has complete dominion over the body of Osiris, according to her wishes, needs and whims.*
d. Without permission from Goddess Ira, it is prohibited for Osiris to have intimate relationships of any kind whatsoever. Osiris is

also forbidden to perform sexual acts with himself unless this is commissioned by Goddess Ira.
e. Osiris shall, without hesitation, be honest and open about his thoughts, feelings and wishes when Goddess Ira asks this. Osiris has no right of privacy. If Goddess Ira makes a request to Osiris, Osiris shall immediately and without restraint answer honestly about every aspect of his life, including his dreams, his thoughts, his fantasies and his knowledge. Goddess Ira shall never punish Osiris for this openness.
f. All that Osiris knows, thinks or writes is available to Goddess Ira.
g. Osiris is obliged to learn those skills that Goddess Ira asks from him. These skills are available to Goddess Ira.
h. Osiris accepts any penalties resulting from disobedience with gratitude. Goddess Ira is not obliged to mention the reason of the punishment.
i. Osiris always refers to Goddess Ira as "Goddess" or "private name" or any other name with which Goddess Ira agrees.
j. Osiris is required to undergo any torture or humiliation. Osiris is not entitled to refuse anything or to stop the torture or humiliation.
k. Osiris shall ensure that he shall visit Goddess Ira regularly.
l. Osiris wears the collar of Goddess Ira as much as possible.
m. Osiris shall, during life and if applicable after her life, act as advisor of Goddess Ira.

Article 4: Obligations Goddess Ira and rights of Osiris.
a. Goddess Ira takes charge of the life of Osiris.
b. Goddess Ira shall help Osiris in the deepening (spiritual, sexual and emotional) of his needs and his knowledge.
c. Goddess Ira ensures that no lasting physical and mental injuries or damage shall occur to Osiris unless jointly agreed.
d. Osiris is entitled to maintain normal etiquette and behavior. Osiris shall also be given the opportunity to carry out his work and his duty as a husband and father. In reference to the household and the family of Osiris there will be nothing required, in any way whatsoever, that would cause any harm to his children or his functioning as father and or husband. If Osiris has intercourse with his wife he shall notify Goddess Ira thereof. Osiris is required, unless

otherwise decided by Goddess Ira, to limit having intercourse with his wife as much as possible.
 e. Goddess Ira, or on request of Osiris, takes care of the fulfilling of the sensual and sexual needs of Osiris.

This agreement is drafted and signed in life, in good (mental) health and, in full and free will of the persons mentioned above. By signing this contract Osiris became wholly owned by Goddess Ira.

Agreed on 9 February 2010

.. ..
Signature of Goddess Ira

... ...
Signature of Osiris

... ...
Signature of Witness: Charlotte

    Charlotte asked you if you understood the contract. You signified your agreement on the stipulations of the contract by verbally stating your acceptance.

    "I accept your desire to serve me and the secrets of your heart written on this paper. I will honor your feelings and needs. I will always put your best interests foremost in my dominance over you. You belong to me, thus you are now a part of my body and soul. Your happiness, health and well being are in my care and I will thoughtfully tend to them because you are a part of me and my destiny."

    Charlotte asked me if I had understood the stipulations of the contract. I signified my agreement by verbally stating my acceptance.

    "I accept the conditions of my service and respect the secrets of your heart written on this paper. I will honor and love you as I serve you to the best of my ability. I will open my heart, body and mind to your will, trusting that you have my best interests in your heart. My submission to you will be a gift freely given and shall never become a burden that I must bear. I am now a part of you and will respect you and your dominance over me as our lives and destinies have become one."

    You removed the bow of my tuxedo and placed the collar around my neck and fastened it securely. You proclaimed: "You now belong to me." And

I answered: "I now belong to you Goddess Ira." On the collar was inscribed consuasor Dea Ira.

This contract was then signed by the three of us and the agreement is safely stored away.

The second major step in the destroying Osiris identity was achieved. He became voluntary my possession.

You then attached the leash to the collar as your commitment to lead and guide me from this day forward. I pressed my lips to Goddess Ira feet to symbolize my respect and submission. I inhaled and enjoyed her delicate fragrance. I remained in this position until you Goddess Ira tugged gently at the leash and "commanded" me to raise my head. You then kissed me and told me to stand. The bells sounded several times to announce the newly formed bond. You embraced me and kissed me again. I was glad that the whole sermon was recorded. It is a kind of marriage you told me. Your gift fulfilled me with an immense gratitude. I was glad that I belonged to my Goddess. My Goddess, who I love, honor, respect and obey for all of eternity.

I wished to give you my Goddess a special gift. The gift should be valuable to me. It was not so easy to make a choice. Almost all my possessions had no emotional value. The gift I received from a grandmother when I rescued her grandchild from a snake would be a good one. She did wear it when she was a young child. It was a symbol of her youth and innocence. It is an appropriate symbol for my newly formed bound with you my Goddess.

I also had a gift purchased form a jeweler. It was a chain on which a key hung. The chain symbolized my servitude to you and the key symbolized that my heart belonged to you my beautiful Goddess.

I was then ordered to undress. I stood naked in front of my Goddess and our witness. The fire marks and my tattoos were clearly visible. Charlotte made beautiful pictures of you and me.

Then you instructed me to lie face down on the ground with arms and legs spread out like a cross. You said: "In receiving the collar you gave up your most precious possession. Yourself. Your Ego. This makes you fit to be ordained as a priest in my cult."

You tied my hands and took me to another room. I had to put my hands over my head. My hands were attached to a pulley. The pulley was pulled up. You walked around me for inspection. Like an owner inspects his goods. You then proceeded to flog me and said that by the collaring "you became my possession, my object. Using this whip underlines this. Your identity has changed fundamentally. You are mine now. I will now baptize you. It is a ritual cleansing and anointing. Will you preserve the privileges of the priestly office and not abuse it?" I answered: "Yes I will."

You ordered me to lie down and you placed your knees at both side of my head and you ordered me to open my mouth so that I received your living water. You were so close that I could smell your lovely scent. No drop of the divine water I wanted to spill. You recited: "You are now born again in body, mind and soul. I order you, unless otherwise instructed, to show in my presence the symbols of my divine status which I have engraved in your body. Your name will be no longer Martin Job but Osiris. Your name signifies that you are an ordained priest in my cult. As my priest your body will be clean shaven from now on." Then you blessed me and part of the prophesies of the voice had been fulfilled. I enjoyed the whole day except the drinking of your nectar but I was nevertheless grateful for this gift I had received. With this gift I received some of your life force.

After the session we went for a lunch to celebrate our newly formed bond. Unfortunately I had to leave you. But before I left you put a ball stretcher around my balls and cock. This ball stretcher you closed with a padlock. I had learned to be obedient.

To have this contract and to actually own a person is a very special thing I am glad we made that commitment .It's a union of trust and loyalty and as a Dominant it is a powerful pact with your chosen sub. This contract is eternal, just as the burn marks, as one does not start this procedure with the intention to end it it's one of the strongest bonds one can have.

3 Dominance of Goddess Ira intensified and submission increased.

When I came to visit again I was an owned and collared man and you stood at the door waiting for me. I noticed that you Goddess Ira were indeed visibly the daughter of Maat. You looked so beautiful and so seductive and you did wear a short black latex dress. I noticed your décolleté which is of an indescribably beauty and I find your tunnel irresistible. In front, at neck height, the right and the left side of your pretty dress was connected with a big band. The front of your dress was a few inches shorter than the back. Under the dress you wore a black latex slip. I couldn't help myself but suddenly I remembered the delicious scent of you. You walked on high heels and wore black latex sleeves. These sleeves started just above your elbows and ran from there to your exquisite hands. In short, your appearance was striking. But as always I was particularly affected by your beautiful face. I greeted you with the Italian word ciao. This expression derived from the Venetian phrase sciao vostro which means "I am your slave" an apt description since the collaring.

I must admit that I had mixed feelings. My heart always melts like a glacier under the hot sun when I see or think about you. I fought that day for the last time with the loyalty I felt towards my wife. I had never before entered a relationship since I was married to my wife. Now I am married twice. I knew that these mixed feelings were the offspring of my ego but the feelings of love and kinship for you were much stronger. I handed over my promised collaring poem to you.

Collaring by Goddess Ira

On the bed I sat meditating
My promises rehearsing
A day full of signification
This day of my resurrection

A bouquet of roses carried
Flowers especially for you selected
A sign of my eternal love
These flowers for my Goddess which I wholly love

A leash was carried in the other hand
I now fall under your command
You held a whip
With the whip you sealed my lip

I gave you my roses of love
They glorify my eternal love
The leash I handed over to you
Token of the guiding I shall receive from you

I knelt down for you
I told you that I adore you
Perpetual promises exchanged
My future secured

My soul wished deeply to be yours
This wish was granted and now I'm yours
You put the collar on
Full property status was done

My mind, body and soul I gave to you
My new identity was given by you
The key of my heart was presented
A new phase was thus initiated

It was a gathering very special
As our common future shall tell
You are my Goddess for who I fell
I'm now embodied in your body and soul

> I will obey and respect you
> I will assist you
> I will fully inform you
> I will serve, honor and above all love you

Osiris

I like to receive poems to honor me, it's something I like when they are displayed nicely and can be shared with others who are visiting my house. I am sure there will be more following so I decided to display it in the central part of my living room. They look smart and are as beautiful to look at as they are to read....

I had a second surprise for you my Goddess. A memorial jewel was specially designed for you. This pendant can be worn two ways and is made of gold and silver. It is elegantly designed and full of symbolism. On the left and right side of the pendant the wings are depicted. They represent the divine status of you Goddess Ira. In the middle polished malachite is incorporated. This stone is carved in the form of a flame and reflects the color of the eyes of you my Goddess. This flame is also a symbol of my rebirth and of my heart that burns for you. Around the base of the flame is a golden circle. This circle commemorates my collaring. If the pendant is turned over the wings appear and in the middle the golden circle. In the middle of this circle my penis is carved out. It confirmed that even my most private part was ceded to you and carries a name which you gave it. It also reflects the black rite. Above the circle is a triangle. This triangle refers to the pyramids of Egypt, Mexico and the secret rite. You thanked me and asked me to put the pendant around your neck. I am always glad when you wear it because it reminds me about our special bond. This memorial jewel is depicted on my phone. Each time I use my phone I see this memorial jewel and I have to think about you and our special relationship. Then you brought me upstairs.

The jewel pleased me as I don't have the habit of wearing jewellery; this one was elegant, small and really well chosen to be worn by me. It fitted my eyes and my tattoos perfectly. I was sure I would wear this gift very often.

I entered the room and halted, awaiting permission to present myself. I lowered my eyes. I was ordered by you to raise my arms and you blindfolded me. A blindfold always gives me a heighted tension because my primary sense is vision. Your hands began slowly to undress me and during this process my entire body was examined, touched and commented upon until I remained standing fully naked with my hands behind my back. I was aroused, exited, nervous and within the complete control of you. You fixed a leash to my collar. I was instructed to assume a crawling position and to crawl toward the feet of you. I was not yet allowed to physically touch you. Finally you allowed me to kiss your toes.

I was then commanded to face toward you on my knees, the thighs opened as wide as possible to display my genitals, shoulders back, hands on the thighs, palms cupped upward, buttocks resting on the heels, chin up and eyes respectfully lowered. You told me that the purpose of the stripping of my clothes and this presentation was to reinforce my status and to remind me that I am owned and dominated by you. This became our standard ritual when I am with you.

Then you ordered me to present for discipline. My hands were cuffed at my collar. You asked me in what way I had violated our agreement. I told you that my first violation was that I have performed sexual acts with myself while I was not commissioned by you. I fantasized that I had sex. While I was fantasizing I was masturbating.

You reminded me that in accordance with our agreement I had no right of privacy. You requested me to answer honestly about every aspect of my life. This included my fantasies. I did as requested and you remarked that I had been honest about my fantasies and that for this you would not punish me. But I will whip you for violating our property agreement. You have performed sexual acts with yourself while I did not commission you. You asked me did you commit more violations.

I answered to you my beloved Goddess that my second violation was that I have not mentioned forthwith that I had sex with my wife and that I didn't describe how we had sex. I violated thus the privacy article of the property agreement.

As his owner I always made sure that Osiris adhered to the property stipulations.

For each of the offences you punished me. You allocated fifteen whippings for each of the offences and at the end of each whipping I had to thank you. I offered you then my buttocks for spanking. Between the spanking and spitting you stroked my penis. Again I was instructed to open my genitals for your inspection. You humiliated and dominated me by discussing the size of my offering. Suddenly you grabbed the back of my head and held it steady. Involuntary I opened my mouth. When my mouth was still open from the scream of agony you spat your saliva into my mouth.

Because it was so difficult to keep my hands from my genitals you would put my equipment in a chastity cage when I went home. You were the key holder and you determined the length of time. You let me see the chastity cage. I saw that the chastity cage consisted of three interlocking pieces that fitted together. Two guide pins hold the top pieces together. The bottom opening of the cage allowed for use at the urinals. The locking pin went through the middle recessed hole connecting the cage portion to the ring. You held several rings in your hand and you explained that the rings were in different sizes and would be used to stretch my balls.

While I was in the discipline position you introduced me to a mistress who is trained by you. She is tall and slender fairly good looking. Her blond hair is half long. She wore a black dress and black latex boots that ended just above her knees.

I was then ordered to sit on my thighs. You stroked my body. Your hands caressed and massaged me. It felt sensual. Then you pinched my nipples lightly. Next you pulled and twisted my nipples and put clamps on them which was painful. Other clamps were put on other parts of my body and at last you put clamps on my vulnerable genitals. You Goddess Ira never forgot to brush the clamps on my nipples which re-sensitized them. I couldn't help myself each time I had to moan and you answered my moaning with one of your lovely smiles. You even trailed the loose clothespin down my stomach and around my genitals. You brushed all the clamps again which caused an eruption of pain at the connected body parts. To say that I had to moan again is an understatement. Finally you unclipped my wrist from the collar and fixed the leash to the collar and toke me to the stretcher.

The third important step in the destruction of the identity of Osiris was his complete mental subjugation to me. This was necessary for the replacing of his Ba, Ka, and Sheut by mine. He was from now on only allowed to focus on me. No room should be left for others or for Osiris himself. I had to control his mind completely.

You tied my body down with multiple straps and my hands were tightly bound to either side of the stretcher. Also my head was tightly fixed via the collar. When you were ready you put a set of headphones on my head. I had to look into the hypnotic lights and I recognized that you made use of subliminal stimuli. Your initial commands were harmless. Relax that is the key. Think less. Look deeper and relax more. But quickly a wave of disorientation swept through me and I lost control. It felt like the sedation in a hospital. There was blackness all around me but far, far away I heard endlessly your instructions and commandments. "You obey me so completely that you have no other way to be. Your commitment to me is untraceable. You believe and feel anything I want you to feel or to believe ...."

The headphones faded into silence and the lights slowed and stopped. I was still lying on the stretcher while you looked at me. However I was still seeing the patterns of lights and hearing the instructions repeating in my head. Then suddenly you asked me for what purpose I exist and I

The Elevation to Divinity

answered: To further the cause of you my Goddess and Owner. Obedience to you is my sole purpose. Loving you is my only possibility. Submitting to your will is my most important task. Your next question was what is your reward? And I answered: Ever increasing levels of pleasure. The higher my level of pleasure the higher my level of surrender Goddess Ira. My head was pounding when I opened my eyes and saw you my Goddess. I realized that I was still lying on the stretcher and you freed me and gave the order to kneel before you. Automatically I said: Yes Goddess Ira your command is my only purpose and you said you have earned a reward. My reward was to inhale your scent. I knelt and inhaled your lovely scent as deep as I could and closed my eyes. Your fragrance was delightful and I still can smell it. For me there is no nicer fragrance then yours.

My flower bomb from Viktor &Rolf is the perfect perfume for me. It agrees with me completely.

The reason I let Osiris smell my scent was something he was not aware of ... When removing the headphones I had slipped in a little device, size of a teardrop, and especially designed for me to psychologically control Osiris thoughts, to hypnotize him. The device is activated by the scent of my perfume. I have placed in Osiris pocket seven small sealed plasticized envelopes, they contain my scent. I will order him on a regular base to smell my scent.

It activates the device slowly and he will start hearing my voice, very softly as if it is just his imagination, when he rests he will hear the voice every half hour and he will only be able to dream about his Goddess that way.

Its mind control and I know I don't need it, but it's new and in an experimental faze and I can't resist this ...I know it will exclude all doubts he has regarding this commitment and his mission.

Being not in a 24/7 BDSM relationship the control is a very important factor to keep the bond between D/s vivid and exciting.

As Osiris is in a relationship I don't want to jeopardize this by sending messages and mails at random, when it suits me. I can imagine that Osiris suffers more to have to leave this part of his life with me here than I do as I live this surreal life here, in my big house with playrooms and toys and playmates a volonté, whilst he has to wear his secrets in his everyday life ..

But he wears them with pride, and my little device will assure me that I won't have to use too much pressure and force to make him the person I want him to be... I know I will change him and all his values will be broken and replaced by my values ...Fortunately for him my values are very respectable and pure!

I will call my little device my rc hypno, just a small aid to succeed in my mental subjugation. I wonder how long it will take Osiris to make the connection between hearing my voice after smelling my scent, I don't think that will take long, but unless he has his ears sprayed he will not know the soft but demanding voice is coming from my rc hypno.

In the missions I have for him in the future this device will be very useful to motivate him and to know his whereabouts as it is also a tracking device ... I will always know his whereabouts, because the mission I have for him to accomplish will take him to places where he will be cut off from any means of communication to the outside world and his Goddess.

In my head I am slowly preparing the scheme of events to follow.....

In time our bond will become so strong that I won't need to brainwash him to purify his thoughts and to clear negative emotions from his soul and his dependence towards me will make this possible . Only a willing soul is a soul one can take, but a soul is a precious thing, the cleaning needs to be done with utmost care whilst the body may be brutalised, the soul always needs to be handled with care.

In time our bond will become so strong that the thought alone will open a morphogenetic field (also called collective field of knowledge) between us where we can read each other's thoughts and share our wisdom and experiences as I am convinced that morphogenetic fields are everywhere around us and if we want to make use of them, all it takes is to train your receptors, not only train them but first make them receptive. I am already very skilled in using the morphic energy to store and download information that I need or that I have stored from one of my previous life's.

I call this "the presence of the past" and by getting older I am more aware of things I simply know and things I suddenly pick up by just showing signs of interest.

The belief in the theory of morphic resonance (by Rupert Sheldrake) challenges the fundamental assumptions of modern science.

All natural systems, from crystals to human society, inherit a collective memory that influences their form and behavior. Because of this cumulative memory, through repetition the nature of things becomes increasingly habitual. Things are as they are because they were as they were.

Rather than being ruled by fixed laws, nature is essentially habitual, and people are no exception, most people are complete habit creatures, so is Osiris, but he will become less and less and spiritual as he already is, his spiritual side will merge with mine and the presence of the past will be shared to serve the higher purpose that we were chosen for.

The Elevation to Divinity

I strongly believe that science and spirituality can and should interact, in order to move beyond the limits of the ordinary, to blend science, creativity, intellectual curiosity and traditional wisdom to explore and expand our views of reality.

In our mission we will investigate the relationships between chaos and creativity and their connection to cosmic consciousness and test them on the cosmic bond we have come to establish between us.

The dreamscapes of our life, that's how this all started for us anyway....

Our combined strength, souls and wisdom and the use of the sources described above will make us invincible and our union indestructible.

It was clear that I Goddess Ira was successful with the mental subjugation of Osiris. But this process had to be continued it was certainly not finished yet.

One thing I remembered clearly out of the blackness it was the secret history a history only known to the high priests. You Goddess Ira had told me that in the earliest ages there was an organized chaos in our solar system and that our history was a representation of the succession from one constellation to another. The constellations had a huge influence on the density of spirit and our evolution process.

When Saturn and Mars reigned life arose from the sea. The earth was hardened and became dryer and smaller. Mars played an important role in this phase. From Mars we inherited the will to dominate over our fellowman. During this period the Gods still lived among men. At the start, man had direct contact via their minds with the Gods. Matter was at this time by far not as dense as we know it today. This was also the time of Maat, Osiris, Horus and you Ira.

I learned that you Goddess Ira were the daughter of Maat and Mars and that you inherited from Mars the characteristics: Dominance, Dangerous, Extreme and Sadistic. From Maat you Goddess Ira inherited the characteristics: Gorgeous, Original and Sophisticated. The existence of you Goddess Ira was kept secret because your mission was to be kept secret. When you spoke about the Maya calendar you confirmed my knowledge about the legend which predicted the end of time. A time that wicked people united in a secret society would try to grasp world domination an event that only could be prevented by the daughter of Maat and her helper Osiris. Only some high priests and some secret society's knew of this legend and of your existence.

When matter became more and more concrete it formed an increasing barrier to the free flow of the cosmic mind. The inner world, the real world, the world of the Gods was no longer accessible to humans. Osiris was the last god-king who reigned over the earth and had contact with humanity. Since then the cosmic mind, the universal consciousness was separated from our individual physical bodies.

You lectured me that the cosmic mind and our thoughts are of a higher reality. Physical objects are merely shadows or reflections of this higher reality. You lectured me that our consciousness has the structure of the stars above us. I learned that because of the increasing density of matter reproduction was not longer possible via the mind for humanity. The result was that the fleshy penis was created. Thus began the cycle of birth, death and rebirth. And because of the almost complete barrier between spirit and matter the human free will came into existence. To break this blockade of the free will, the ego had to be abandoned if one desired to reach the higher state of consciousness.

Only the high priests knew the secret doctrine and honored since ancient times you Goddess Ira in the black rite. The high priests knew how they could use the conscious thought of the forces of death and sexuality to break down the barrier and to achieve again the higher state of consciousness. I learned that spirituality and sex were indistinguishable. And that the expression of sexual drive went far beyond the individual. It had nothing to do with free will. You told me that the desire for that special person came from a time long before our conception. In essence sexual desire is spiritual and sacred and should be treated as such. Every time when you have sex the cosmic constellation is involved. If love is practiced you interact with the vast cosmic powers. And if you decide to do that consciously it is a magic deed. Through certain rituals that situation can be achieved. It is known as the black rite. You told me that if two people use the secret knowledge and become one then you break through the barrier and you can create the future ". Intercourse in a traditional way is not necessarily required during the black rite but love is."

Knowledge of this secret doctrine could only be acquired via an inner journey. Several initiations let by you Goddess Ira had to be performed by the suitable chosen applicants. It is a dangerous and extreme journey in which you encounter the dark and demonic depths of yourself and of the universe. This could only be done through experiencing the worst life has to offer. It is wrestling with your own demons and complete letting go of your own ego and free will. It is travelling to the other side of madness. I had to change fundamentally the bottom of the pit had to be reached to acquire the skills to create the future with you.

The Egyptian population was only allowed in the outer courts of the temple. They were only familiar with the Osiris story in as far as it was related to the fertility myth. This myth was an allegory based on the flooding of the Nile which made the land fertile. But the higher significance of the allegory was only known to the high priests. The existence and huge importance of Goddess Ira was not known at all to the Egyptian population. These secrets were kept inside the temple and were only known to a select company of high priests.

Now I better understood the treatments I received from you Goddess Ira. Your treatments were designed to break down my ego. My identity had to be faded out and replaced by your identity. To achieve that desired result I had to be completely dominated by you Goddess Ira. This was a prerequisite. Only then I could be the helper described in the legend of the Maya. The tattoo of the snakes of the caduceus in my pubic flashed through my mind when I thought about the two contradictory principles Domination and submissiveness.

But the domination is a must to accomplish what we started. Why was I chosen to fulfill a sacred mission in this life now? Without guidelines to what or how? The knowledge is within you, that's all I had to go on... I consulted some stored information from the morphic source about rituals and rites and older cultures, with the easiness that others surf online with by using Google, and combined them with my other highly developed skills and that is the power of domination …

You instructed me to lie on a bench. You tied me down. Again I got a blindfold and you put a gag in my mouth. I could no longer utter a sound. You sat on my face and I could hardly breathe. While you sat on my face I felt that you stuck something in my urethra. Then you my beloved Goddess left the room and I could breathe again. I was relieved but that was only for a short period. The thing that you had stuck into my urethra dripped and it felt hot. Suddenly I understood what was happening you had stuck a candle in my urethra. I started to sweat and prayed that you would come back very soon. Although I was blindfolded I knew that it would be a matter of seconds that the candle was burning inside my penis. Then you came into the room and started to laugh hard. You teased me. Shall I blow it out? I tried to nod but I failed. You said because you are not clear in your answer I have to teach you to be clear I will pierce your tongue. It had than become so hot that I didn't care what would happen. I was only grateful that you

Goddess Ira and Osiris

blew out the candle. You ordered me to stick out my tongue. With a scissor in your left hand you pulled out my tongue a little further and with your right hand you pierced my tongue. It did hurt. You also stretched my Prince Albert piercing and also that did hurt. It was stretched to 3, 4 millimeter.

After piercing my tongue and penis I had to lay down with my head faced to the ground and you then put on the chastity cage and locked it and I went back home. When I was home I pulled as instructed my phone out of my pocket. Put the ear buds in my ear and pressed play. It wasn't music I heard it was the voice of you. "Osiris lives to obey the will of Goddess Ira. Each moment that passes Osiris surrenders more completely to me. The goals of Goddess Ira are the goals of Osiris. The desires of Goddess Ira are the desires of Osiris. Osiris mind and body are the property of Goddess Ira. Osiris does not question but obeys. To obey is pleasure. Osiris is addicted to Goddess Ira. Your inner mantra is: "Obey Goddess Ira. To obey her is pleasure."

Those earphones were used to confuse Osiris in a positive way, the lines he heard were the lines he has been hearing for the past weeks, but unaware, this action will make his believe in our "pact" become only stronger and stronger.

I no longer moved. My eyes didn't see. They were blank. I slowly knelt. I trembled from the pleasure that even the simple hearing of the inner mantra brought to me. I was hungry for more. Commands began to enter my mind while I was kneeling. I am so conditioned that I as often as I can I listen to your commands. I cannot tell any longer the difference between the thoughts that were mine and the thoughts I was fed by you. This is the way I have to think and to respond. I have no choice. The instructions overwhelmed every thought, every emotion. It stimulated and still stimulates my pleasure centers in wave after wave with an intensity that cannot be matched. The mind control of you Goddess Ira reprogrammed my psyche. There is only mindless obedience to you. I am craving for the pleasure you give me. The pleasure is securely nested in my motivational center. I am conditioned to do the will of you Goddess Ira. The will of my Goddess. Each time I listened to the phone, I said the inner mantra and I trembled with ecstasy. The dam had burst open. I surfed on the waves of orgasm after orgasm. Pleasure is now strongly anchored with your commands. Your commands became me and I thought that my ego was completely gone.

You see, my actions had the result I was hoping for. I could say for this part "mission accomplished" but still I did not want to remove my rc hypno yet, I made a decision to leave it in until the full mission had been brought

The Elevation to Divinity

to a successful end ... and I must admit I do enjoy reading Osiris reports on how he feels I control his mind and thoughts, how he is filled with this new emotion how he is able to enter what I offered: a new understanding of life, matter and mind.

Since then I am completely devoted to you. It is almost impossible to work or do other things and not to think of you. Since that time I am completely dominated by you and my submission was almost complete I had no free will left. Or was there still a little bit of my ego left?

My aim was the mental subjugation of Osiris. I had reached an important milestone. Osiris focused from now on only on ME.

Responsible preparation and collection of the holy objects.

4 Dangerous Goddess Ira.

On my next visit you looked as always fantastic. You wore one of my favorite outfits a short black skirt and a black top. These clothes gave justice to your beautiful breast and legs and your face was made up in a way that I find breathtaking. You wore the pendant. The ring with the carved out cock was clearly visible.

Like the other times I entered the room and waited for permission to present myself. I lowered my eyes, raised my arms and you blindfolded me. Your hands began slowly to undress me and during this process my entire body was examined, touched and commented upon until I remained standing fully naked with my hands behind my back. In the presence of you my Goddess I was of course aroused and exited. A leash was fixed to my collar and again I was commanded to face toward you on my knees, my thighs opened as wide as possible to display my genitals, shoulders back, hands on the thighs, palms cupped upward, buttocks resting on the heels, chin up and my eyes respectfully lowered. I worshiped and loved you my Goddess very much. You were a miracle of beauty and grace.

With the leash in your hand you brought me to another room were you put me in a black body bag and put a black latex hood over my head. I couldn't move any longer. You opened the body bag at the places where my nipples were and started to play with them. You also opened the body bag were my cock was and put my prick in letter harnesses and fixed ropes at my Prince Albert piercing. You were having fun with your helpless property. Time and time again you pulled with force at the ropes. Of course this did hurt. After that you put a steel tube in my urethra to stretch it. But the treatment was not over yet; you put an artificial cunt over my penis and put

The Elevation to Divinity

on the vibrator. I could not prevent that I had an orgasm. Then Goddess Ira girded my penis with a locked chastity device. The tattooed eye of Horus embraced with your kiss and the caduceus were clearly visible. While I was lying helplessly in the black body bag you lectured me with your wonderful voice about the cosmic order and about reality.

I said to Osiris that the experience of the will comes from the fact that our actions follow our desires. Free will is emotion. It is an illusion. Man lives in an ego tunnel. In essence, the self is a myth. Man is an ego machine.

The ego is a tool that has evolved by predicting his behavior and by understanding the behavior of others. Each of us lives his or her life in his or her own ego tunnel. That's why I put you in a latex body bag and put a hood on your head. Do you see the similarity? You cannot move out of the restricted area. You have no direct contact with me when I touch you. Because of this ego tunnel we have no direct contact with the external reality. But we do possess an inner perspective. Each of us has a self-conscious model that is rooted in emotions and physical sensations. It is his or her core experience. It is you. How can you escape your ego tunnel? How can you escape from you? This can only be achieved by real unity with another individual. The cup must be empty; otherwise the cup can't be filled. It is the ego that makes us full of ourselves. We must let the ego go. It is my duty to change your ego completely. Remember your body; soul and mind belong to me. They are fused with me. To love you is to love me. To be you is to be a part of me. My ego tunnel has to become your ego tunnel.

I have told you Osiris that the entire universe is represented by energies and states of consciousness that are always present in everything. We are, like all life, like all matter and energy, part of this cosmic energy. Sometimes the cosmic energy is called universal love. We can activate this source by earthly love. However this has to be done with the right intentions. Honesty and good intentions are a prerequisite. If it is done the right way you will by your own sensual spirituality be more complete. The ancient way of becoming part of the universal love is to achieve ecstasy. In an ecstatic state life energy flows through the seven centers of the body and we are in full contact with the cosmic energy. A higher state of consciousness is the result. Ecstasy is healing and removes the obstacles. If you do this in the correct way you will enjoy life much more. You break with self-imposed or culturally specific restrictions, such as guilt or shame. It means that you voluntary and completely surrender to other persons. It means giving up your ego. If you do, then there is both ecstasy and real unity. Nothing is then impossible. Together you become creators.

Since I am a Goddess I had already achieved that lofty state and I did lead and train Osiris. He had to learn to work with his body without shame or guilt. He had to accept his body and the needs of his body and mind and those of others. Only by surrendering to another person or persons he can escape from his ego tunnel."

After this lecture I shackled his ankles with an iron chain and Osiris hands were tied with a rope behind his back. A long chain was connected to his shackled ankles. I then went to the adjoining room where I pressed a button. The result was that Osiris slowly was pulled up at his ankles and via a specially built rail system he was transported to the room where I was.

The time had come to proceed with my mission. I had to fulfill my destiny. I knew that it wouldn't be easy since certain secret societies wanted at all cost to avoid the success of my mission. It would be also dangerous for Osiris. He had to travel to Japan, Egypt and Mexico. This secret society had spread her tentacles all over the world. This secret society had become part of government organizations and international organizations a formidable adversary.

At that time I couldn't tell Osiris what the grave danger was since he was physically or mentally not ready yet. He had to be further prepared to be able to endure pain and humiliation. As said earlier, his ego has to fade out completely into my ego because he has to trust me completely at the end of my quest. For his training it was important that I found a suitable partner for him. It was also important that I maintained the control over Osiris even if I was not physically present. I had to know at any time what was happening. That's why I gave him the order that if he was carrying out my orders or if he breached the ownership agreement he had to report it in detail to me.

New scientific developments made maintaining a remote watch on Osiris however easier. Osiris was still hanging with his head down at the rail. I took a small surgical knife and made an incision just below the chin and grabbed a tiny chip. I wiped the few drops of blood away with a tissue and hide the chip in the freshly made incision. I told Osiris that this chip was a little microphone. Again I took the little knife this time I made an incision at the place where the sixth chakra resides. I told him that this chip was a tiny camera. If you look very carefully at Osiris you can see a little blue dot. Under his balls I made an incision and put a chip there too. This chip would always tell me where he was.

The final incision was low in his back, near the tailbone. There I put an internal processor which was the size of two sticks of gum. I said to Osiris stimulating in this exact place shoots pleasure signals through your nervous system straight up to the part of your brain that processes information coming from the genitals. The external part of the processor I held in my hand, it was roughly the size of a belt pager. With this device I could decide when Osiris had an erection and how powerful his ejaculations would be. I put on the device and cranked it up to maximum. His penis immediately became an angry snake and his rectal muscles squeezed rhythmically in time with the pulses even before the orgasmic finale. After these orgasms Osiris was exhausted and I put him down and put the chastity belt on him.

I told Osiris that the modern word "prostitution" with its negative connotations from sex and the porn industry was entirely different than what "sacred prostitution" meant in ancient times. Sex against payment has a negative connotation because of the exploitation and mistreatment of women and man. Prostitution is wrong if the result is a damaged or inferior ego. A prostitute should insist that she or he is well-treated. There should be mutual trust and respect. I narrated that temple prostitution was an instrument to break down the ego and it had a sacred purpose.

Prostitution was used like this in the original temple prostitution. The office of the temple priestesses or temple priest was about the unity of body and mind, and sex was a spiritual experience. In this unity there was direct contact with the Goddess. The priestess and priest were instruments and sex was a ritual to obtain this unity. This was in essence what they called the black rite. If persons were properly trained and became truly one they could blend the cosmic energy and create what they wish. After that I sent him home to wait for further instructions and to listen as often as he could to my sublimal affirmations on his pone. The process of mind control had to be continued.

These affirmations were:

- *You obey me completely*
- *You exist to further my cause*
- *Obedience is your purpose*
- *Loving me is your only possibility*
- *Submitting to my will is your task*
- *Code word: deep hypnosis/trance*
- *Your reward: increasing levels of pleasure*
- *The higher the pleasure the higher the surrender*
- *My command is your purpose*
- *Each moment you surrender more to me*
- *To obey me is pleasure*
- *Inner mantra: to obey me is pleasure*
- *Your believe and feel anything I want*
- *Your soul, mind and body are mine*
- *You are my property*
- *You belong to me*

The Elevation to Divinity

I did as you my Goddess had instructed. These affirmations are now completely ingrained in my mind. They became part of my altering ego.

I gave Osiris the instruction to be at a particular time at a designated carpool site. I mentioned that the assignment was important for his further development and I had to test him how sincere he was. It would be a lesson in humiliation. He had to learn to be subordinated to the woman. This would be the fourth step in the destruction of Osiris identity. He would not see me.

As expected, he obeyed me. A friend of mine picked him up. The agreed code was exchanged. My friend blindfolded him and started the engine. When the engine stopped she told him that he had to enter the private club across the street. In this club he had to choose one of the presented girls and to render to her my envelope.

From Osiris I learned later that he felt quite uncomfortable when he entered the club. The hostess presented seven girls. I noticed via the implanted chips that it was difficult for him to choose. He did choose a tall slender girl named Honey. She had a Javanese appearance and almond-shaped eyes. He gave her the envelope with which she walked away. In the mean time I observed that his nervousness increased. He didn't know what I had written. Meanwhile, the girl read my note.

"The person in front of you is my property. He is my personal slave. That's why he wears my collar and my Prince Albert piercing. I have instructed him to go to your club and to choose one of the girls. He chose you. The instructions in this letter are not known to him. The intention is that you make him your prostitute. In this envelope is 50 euro. You are his customer and pay him the 50 euro. He is your whore. You are in charge and you decide what he has to do. However it is forbidden for him to have sex with you. He may not penetrate you. In the envelope was also the key of the chastity cage. It was important for me to see if the girl would adhere to my instructions. If so, she could be a suitable companion.

I also had written that I would appreciate it if she could tell me briefly what she had done with my property and what she thought of his performance.

I had ordered Osiris to send me a report about his experience. The next day Osiris sent me a detailed report about the experience he had with Honey.

He wrote: Honey brought me to the Roman room she gave me 50 euro and Honey said: **"I'll pay you 50 euro because you will be today my whore. I want you to massage me, lick me, suck me and after that I'll**

fuck you with a strap-on dildo." She instructed me to undress and to wash. While she watched me closely I gave extra attention to my genitals and to my armpits. Then she took a washcloth and washed her pussy. After this we both rinsed our mouth. I felt to the core humiliated and very tense.

Honey told me that she was a novice BDSM Dominatrix. Honey was tall and slender, her breasts were firm but not large and her pussy was shaved. She had three tattoos one high on the upper left arm, one just above her right ankle and the other low on the back just above her buttocks. She also had three piercings. Two piercings through her nipples and one piercing through her clitoris. I found her a friendly nice person with a beautiful face and a great lightly colored body. She was nice to talk to which put me more at ease.

After we undressed she lay on the bed and I anointed her back with oil. I could see that Honey looked with interest at my penis in the chastity cage. Carefully and a little awkward I began to caress her. I massaged her back, buttocks and legs.

Although Honey is a beautiful woman my mind was certainly at the start with you my beloved Goddess. I was full of questions. The most important question I had was why you did do it? Why did you insist that I made love with another woman? I loved you and one of the affirmations was that loving you was my only possibility. Of course I understood that sex couldn't be equated with love. But I also knew that I had to obey you completely and that I had to cede to your wishes.

Anyway after some time she turned and I started to massage her front. Her nipples were hard my hand went first to her breasts and then to her stomach. My mouth searched for her right nipple and started sucking it gently. But I thought at the beautifully sculptured breast of my Goddess. How I would love to see and to suck her nipples. Suddenly I remembered what you had said at the collaring ceremony "You belong to me, thus you are now a part of my body and soul." In a way I envisioned that her nipples become your nipples. Was it my imagination or was it actually happening that when I had these thoughts the nipples of Honey stiffened even more? With the right hand I caressed her left breast and started to suck her left nipple as well. After that I took my time to massage and to kiss her smooth belly, her hairless legs and thighs. Honey became you and you became Honey.

Finally my hand slid towards her recently shaved public lips. Her pussy was wonderfully smooth. My tongue went over her nipples and turned laps and went into slow sipping. My finger glided over her public lips and I pressed my finger between them. She was a bit damp. Very gently I rubbed my finger between the genital lips a little further and further while looking for her delight nodule. I am not very experienced because I had to ask Honey where her clitoris was. It was an awkward moment but her clitoris had nevertheless swollen.

I went with my lips over her lips. My middle finger began gently to rub her clitoris. Soft moans echoed through the room covered with mirrors. She raised her knees so that I could lie with my head between her legs. I gently pushed her outer lips so that I could stroke her clitoris and labia softly. My warm tongue, with an easy rhythm, gently liked her lips and penetrated her silken cave and went slowly over and around her clitoris. Her pussy became wetter and wetter from my saliva and her secretion. She tasted delicious like the taste of honey. I caressed her constantly while licking her back and forth. I started to finger her more. Increasingly she began to rotate her hips and I had a beautiful view of her pussy. My tongue was deep inside her pussy and run in circles. I licked her like a dog. Sometimes it was hard to breath. The tip of my nose went up and down on her clit. I kept a steady rhythm going. She became more exited and tasted sweeter. It tasted like "nectar" and smelled more and more musky almost fruity. I could see that she felt hot. Then you Goddess Ira pressed the remote control. My cock responded immediately but was of no use in the chastity device. Honey knew that I wanted to have sex with her. But actually I wanted only to have sex with you. When I almost reached an orgasm you my Goddess used the remote control. I regretted it but in a way I was also relieved. You are the only one for me although I am well aware that I am your property and you can do with me what you want. But even though I had that strong feeling of attachment to you there was still a part of me that wanted to have sex with Honey I was turned on but also Honey didn't allow me to have sex with her. She was the customer and I the whore.

Then Honey ordered me to lick and suck a huge strap-dildo. I did clumsy as ordered. After that she decided to fuck me with the strap-dildo. But she saw that I feared the huge cock and removed the huge strap-dildo. Then it was time and the session ended and I had to take a letter from Honey in a closed envelope to you Goddess Ira.

She wrote to me: "**He understood the command. He has been my whore and did most of the things that belongs to this profession. He did: massage, licking and piping (strap-dildo). But fucking with the strap-dildo failed. His cock stayed in the chastity device. He knows that**

I report directly to you and that motivated him to do more his best. All in all a good slave. Honey"

He had learned to be subordinated to the woman. He had become the whore of a whore. Of course this was an immense blow to his self-worth and destruction of his (manly) identity. However I was not completely satisfied. The strap-dildo failed and the massage could be better. I had to train him further. His ego had to be demolished further and he needed to be trained well to be able to take part in the black rite. It was necessary that during the black rite he completely surrenders to feel the bliss of real unity. For me it was clear that his sexuality and mentality had to be changed a lot more.

A few days after his visit to Honey, Osiris visited me. I was dressed in a short black latex skirt. My breasts were accentuated by thin white stitching. I wore surgical black gloves. I had chosen for this occasion high black boots. It was a rather hot day. I disrobed him and he had to sit in the usual way with his genitals exposed. It's as you know by now one of my ways to make clear to Osiris who is in charge. As agreed in the ownership agreement Osiris was completely smooth.

Mistress Juno entered the room. She is 5 feet tall and has blue-gray eyes. She has long blond hair and a good figure. She was dressed from head to toe in a black latex outfit. I tied the feet of Osiris onto the stretcher. With a thick needle I increased the hole in his dick and fixed a thick piercing ring on his phallus. He groaned in pain and tried to escape. But Mistress Juno pressed his feet against her latex pussy. Osiris told me later that he enjoyed that. Her pussy felt warm he mentioned at that time. From the corner of my eye I saw that Mistress Juno enjoyed also the spectacle. While Osiris was tied I put a vibrator in his ass.

I placed on his nipples piercings that were shaped like horseshoes. Next I connected a big iron bicycle chain with the three piercings and with the ring of the collar. Subsequently I hooded him and put, besides the cock piercing, a dick plug into his urethra.

That day was an important session. I wanted to see how his penis would look like if I modeled it a bit further and to continue the training of Mistress Juno. I began by placing a ball splitter which I significantly tightened. The brandings and tattoos were prominently displayed and had healed nicely. His penis was by now pretty long since it was stretched by the iron chain with the nipples and the ring of the collar. It was an ideal place for my name. As Goddess Ira I had chosen today to use a pencil. At the basis of his cock in a half circle I wrote down with a black pencil my name in Japanese characters. I liked it but Osiris didn't. My sadistic nature enjoyed it. If his penis is excited it can be noticed that his cock is mine. In my vision I had seen how it had to be done and where.

However the modeling of his phallus was still incomplete. It is not for nothing that I gave him the name Osiris. The penis of Osiris has in the ancient legends a particular symbolism. In the future this deserved further attention. His penis must be perfect. First I fixed a double ball stretcher between his cock and his balls. But it had to be stretched more. So I put a second ball stretcher between his cock and his balls. Between the two ball stretchers there was an open space. I tightened the ball splitter further. It was clear that Osiris was in severe pain. Juno had also fun and her eyes sparkled. But I was not yet finished in the space between the ball stretchers I stuck needles into his flesh which came out at the other side. The same I did with the top of his cock. The blood trickled from his genitals where the needles had been stuck. Finally I put on the top of his penis a CBT ring. I turned on the screws and I saw that also this hurt badly. To humiliate Osiris further I invited the husband of Mistress Juno into the room and to look at the results of our craftsmanship.

Mistress Juno and her husband left the room and I was again alone with Osiris. I decided to free him. He stood completely naked in front of me with his three piercings. I decided to fix a rope through his three piercings. He had to bend slightly over. After I had fixed the ropes with the piercings and his collar I ordered him to walk upright. The leash I had in my hand. Of course walking in this position was very uncomfortable. In this way the piercings were in a natural way stretched. I told Osiris: "Dominance seems often to attract those that confuse dominance with power misused… it is not like that …. Imagine the best teacher, boss, sports captain… whoever … did they lead by yelling? Or by bringing out your best and you WANTING to be even better for them?"

Then I brought Osiris to the bathroom. I turned on the shower and ordered him to lie on the ground. I turned off the shower and stood above him. Then I pushed my panties to one side so that my vulva was partly visible for Osiris. While I was standing right above him I started to cascade my nectar on his penis and his body. Pee drinking is one of the things most people would only do if forced by extreme circumstances. For me it was at that time important to see how far he obeyed me. To what extent he was mine. Osiris had told me that he didn't like drinking my nectar. But I knew that champagne drinking has the power to transform the deepest beliefs. I had to effectuate that he craves to drink my golden shower to transform his deepest beliefs. In the end there couldn't be any hesitation and he had to be addicted to it. It was a gradual process that had to be repeated to change his deepest beliefs.

Pee drinking in India dates at least 5000 years back. To drink my nectar was to accelerate Osiris progress towards spiritual enlightenment. I ordered Osiris to open his mouth and to drink my liquid. Which he did and it was the first time after the collaring sermony. What I released and what Osiris recaptured was my life force (prana or chi). Osiris had to be completely saturated by me his Goddess. With the drinking of my nectar I conferred godlike levels of awareness and vitality to Osiris. Besides this certain nutrients were in my urine which were vital to the body's healthy functioning. But drinking urine of a woman impacts the hormonal chemistry of the male body. I used my golden shower also as an instrument to diminish and to suppress his male hormones because he has to become my Egyptian soul. My diet played of course a huge role in the flavor. I knew he loved me very much and that he wanted me to succeed in my divine mission. He who asks about "why" to live can bear almost any "how" to live. He told me that my nectar was somewhat salty. He was sorry to leave me but duty called. He left with the usual expression ciao. At the gate of the garden he yelled to me that he loved me and missed me already. I was aware that he loved me to the core of his being. Without that love I couldn't have continued his training. His love anchored his complete submission to me. Nevertheless he had to prove it time and time again when I tested him further. During these tests his mental restrictions changed and disappeared into the direction which I had mapped out for him. It took time to destroy his ego but he had to become my Egyptian soul in the end. My norms and values became more and more his.

A few weeks later I gave a bag to Osiris. He had to hand over the bag to Honey. In the bag was a sealed envelope and in this envelope was the key of his chastity device. Since he had visited me the last time he did wear this locked chastity device. My instructions for Honey were that she treated Osiris as her personal whore. I wrote to her that she had total permission from me his Goddess to do with him whatever she wanted. I made it clear that I had instructed Osiris that he had to spoil her before the chastity belt could be unlocked. I also gave her permission to have sex with my property. I knew that his mind and feelings were opposed to that thought. No doubts about his subjection to the woman should exist in the future. He had to accept that he was the whore of a whore. By accepting this subjection to the woman his male identity and other restrictions he still had were ready for further destruction.

Goddess Ira and Osiris

I expected that Honey would be able to break down his ego tunnel a bit further. The instrument of repetition makes the changing of norms and values easier. The degeneration of becoming the whore of a whore had great impact on the personality of Osiris. I knew that he originally had strong views about prostitution but I knew that if you became a prostitute you had to break down self-imposed or cultural restrictions. In the view of Osiris and in the view of most people to be the whore of a whore is the ultimate degradation. It was inevitable that my assignment changed Osiris's personality and his views of the world. This inner journey was part of a sophisticated treatment for Osiris that would end in Mexico. He had to be dependent on Honey and to develop emotions for her which conflicted with the strong emotions which he felt for me. But I knew that under all circumstances he regarded himself as my enduring property and that he loved me above everybody else. I knew that even if I wed him in the future to another Goddess, female slave or female switch which belongs to my household this shall not change because I know that he desires from the core of his being that I always will have the Absolute Total Power over him. I know that I have the power to change his personality fundamentally, to take his life and to give life in more than one way. For now I would keep these thoughts in my mind for later consideration. This experience to be the prostitute of a prostitute was to some extent for him the bottom of the pit.

In the bag was also a gift. It was a book about tantra. I knew that she needed to acquire more knowledge about this subject. My last words to Osiris were a warning. Remember that I am in all women. Treat them as you would like to treat me. What you do for them you do for me. But remember also that I want a detailed report from you. I will not accept omissions.

Osiris did as I had ordered and he made a detailed report: When I met Honey I gave her the bag of you my Goddess. Honey read your instructions and started forthwith with the execution of your orders. Honey ordered me to undress. There I stood completely naked before her with only the chastity belt on. She paid me again 50 Euros and told me that henceforth I would be her personal whore. I had still strong objections. To be one time a whore was already one time too much and hardly bearable. To become permanently her whore went much too far and was against all my values. But she made it clear to me that I had no choice. I still refused. To proof her point she let me read a part of the letter of you my Goddess. You wrote explicitly that only you could make an end to this new relationship. I felt I must admit embarrassed, used and angry. But Honey had been right I had no choice if I wanted to obey you and I did acknowledge that I had to obey you.

We both were sitting naked on the bed and were smoking cigarettes. From now on I was her personal whore. Honey could do with me what she wanted. I had to obey my Goddess. Honey wanted me to pamper her and ordered me to start with a massage since the hands of a man are not only destined for masturbation.

Honey handed me a bottle of oil and lay on her belly. I heated the oil in my hands and spread the oil with my hands on the back of her body. I liked to get it spread evenly before I could start rubbing and stroking. I started with her feet and ran up along her legs and torso all the way to her fingertips. I repeated it on the left side of her body. My palms went parallel along the back to her buttocks where I let slip my hands to the sides of her waist and from there up to her shoulders. Then I put the outside of my hands just below the neck and they slipped both sides of the spine down below her waist. When I arrived there I used my thumbs to make small circles on both sides of her backbone all the way up to the shoulders. I also used both my hands alternately in a pulling motion down the sides of her body in the direction of the spine. All of this I did very gently. I saw that her body responded nicely to my caresses. How I wished it would have been you my beloved Goddess. She glanced sideways and saw that my penis was fighting its cage. You used the remote control and my cock became even more violent. When I saw this in the mirror I had to laugh. I did not forget to treat her small buttocks as well.

Groaning she turned on her back and her little sexy tits became visible for me. I could see the hardness of her nipples. My eyes were drawn to her nipples and her luscious mound. Again I heated the oil in my hands and spread the oil with my hands on the front of her body. When I ran my hands from her feet to her knees she shuddered in anticipation. Honey tried to keep her eyes closed but she couldn't help but peek at me her whore. As she looked she noticed that my cock was fighting in its prison. You put the device on maximum. Honey moaned softly as my hands slid up to rub her thighs. Her moaning and your device were driving me wild. I sensed your presence. I envisioned you in front of me. Her nipples were now rock solid. I started to massage her nipples and took them in my mouth to nibble on them. If it were possible her nipples just got harder. With my tongue I fondled her nipples

I could begin to see some wetness. She definitely was turned on. My hands slipped a little lower. She spread her legs slightly to give me a better view. She was also this time cleanly shaven. I loved to get my lips on that, nice smooth little flower. Honey told me that she loved to be totally bare there. She made me a compliment that I had no hair on my genitals and on my crotch. I wanted her. I wanted her badly. No to be more precise I wanted you and I remembered your words "what you do for them you do for me" She was obviously wet and excited. My hands were sliding lower. She was holding her breath in anticipation as my hands dipped low onto her stomach. She reached up and directed my hands were she wanted them. I was not resisting. She spread her legs wide open. Her labia were quite swollen. She moaned in total delight as I slided my fingers down to touch her lips. At her triangle I let the oil drip between my fingers. I was now passionately kissing her all over her body and on her mouth. Our tongues played as butterflies together.

I felt her wetness and I loved it. I really wanted to taste her recently shaved cunt to be more precisely your treasure. I saw her face contorted in pleasure and I wanted to make it last. I placed a finger inside her and felt for her G-spot. I rubbed the outside with my other hand to give her double pleasure. I loved to watch her face. I had to taste her. I run my tongue up and down her luscious labia minora and I shoved my tongue in as far as it would go. I loved to feel her juices on my face. I wanted to make her moan in pleasure. I wanted to make you moan in pleasure. My heart was beating fast. We lay together in the spoon position while I massaged her breast and labia from behind. I felt almost completely content and felt that all boundaries between us had disappeared. I was one with Honey and You. My ego tunnel didn't exist for a short period a new experience for me. I was glad. It looked like eternity. No, we were eternity.

Honey unlocked my chastity device. She took the key out of the envelope and unlocked the lock. The easiest part was the removing of the penis cage. However removing the ring around my balls was a lot more difficult and more painful. My balls had to be squeezed. I made a soft cry when the ring was removed. She liked it, this feeling of power.

Honey asked me to lie on my back. She massaged my chest and stomach very gently. Finally she went to sit at my feet and put her knees up to her chin. She remarked to me I like your tattoo in your pubic region. She also found the eternal kiss there of you gorgeous. She told me that she would also like to have a tattoo just above her clitoris.

It was great to look at her when she sat there with her knees put up to her chin. She had slender shapely legs. And all of this was lightly colored. She looked unlike you the epitome of innocence. Then she gave me a perfect blowjob. She kneeled between my legs and blew my manhood into life. It was a very sexy and a very lusty scene when I peeped at the large mirrors.

She moved rhythmically toward my groin. Her hand fondled my balls and my anus. At the cadence of her lips she squeezed my balls hard and soft. When she kissed my penis she looked deeply into my eyes. I lost myself and was drowning in a pool of brown water which turned into a beautiful green collar the collar which matched the collar of the eyes of my Goddess. Methodically inch by inch she licked my penis. Finally her lips surrounded my cock. When she felt that I would come she used her two fingers to stop the ejaculation process. For more than one hour I was at the brink of an explosion. The boundaries had again disappeared I hoped she would never stop. But she did.

I wanted for a third time to be one with you. I looked at her pleadingly and said that my Goddess said that it was OK as long as my ego would not benefit. I am your hooker so my ego can't benefit. I was so very relaxed and pleased. Finally she let herself be persuaded and said come into me I want to feel you.

As I lay on my back, she took my bare penis in her long slim hands and guided my cock inside her. Rhythmically she started to move her beautiful body up and down my shaft. After a while we swapped positions. She was lying on her back and I noticed that the bones of her pelvis were beautifully cut and visible below the skin I kissed her mouth again and again while she let me inside her treasure. There was a knock at the door. We had rented the room for two hours and those hours had expired. I than started moving fast up and down as I kissed her all over and drowned in her beautiful dark brown eyes. I was in trance I wanted her; no I wanted you very badly. I wanted to be one with her, no you, again to merge with you and to lose myself. Time no longer existed for us. Suddenly we together came. I told Honey that I was very glad that she had given me this special gift and that she would never be the same again for me. She was part of me and I had become part of her. Is that what you meant with your remark, remember what you do for them you do for me?

Honey fixed the ring of the chastity belt around my balls. It hurt a little. Finally, my penis was put back into its cage and the chastity belt was locked by Honey. She kept the key. Hurriedly we dressed and I was sorry to leave.

I did send my report to you Goddess Ira. However, I had not realized enough that you were able through the implanted chips to follow most of what had happened. You told me that my rapport was in accordance of what you had heard and seen and you complimented me with my report. You told me that it was not by chance that you had put on the remote control at that particularly moment.

Although I was not dissatisfied about the progress of Osiris, much remained to be done. Deep emotional ties had been forged. That had been one of my goals. Honey will always be part of Osiris since they have been really one identity. The boundaries of Osiris had shifted. He had accepted the fact that he was her whore. In accordance with his old values and standards he had been the victim of the ultimate degradation. That he as her whore had pleaded to have sex with her and that he had even enjoyed his orgasm with her was important for the destruction of his identity. He had done this voluntarily for me.

However there were still some mental limitations. There were still self-imposed or cultural restrictions. They had to be removed completely. He had to encounter more demons before the black rite could take place. I had to elaborate the idea that life is suffering. I knew Dewi very well. She is a priestess of Vajravan Buddhism. I enlisted her help. Dewi told me that she had seen me on my quest when she was briefly illuminated. She came with one of her followers to Europe to help me with my mission. With her help and the help of Honey I trained and conditioned Osiris further. I hoped that after this training he would be ready for the black rite.

Vajravan Buddhism is based on the idea that "life is suffering". The only way to escape this suffering is to escape the cycle of rebirths and to cease existing altogether. Vajravan Buddhism involves esoteric visualizations, symbols and complicated rituals. It lays great emphasis on magic. In Vajrayana traditions there is no external point for good and evil. Some of its adherents strive to transform erotic passion into spiritual ecstasy.

Followers of Vajravan Buddhism are taught not to suppress their desires but to indulge in them. One is taught not to reject and deny desires but rather to transcend them. Sometimes you have to experience desires in order to realize the inherent emptiness in the senses. Once emptiness is realized, accepting or rejecting them is also empty.

I send instructions to Osiris and Honey to meet Dewi at my place.

At the designated date and time Honey and Osiris came to my place. I noticed when they arrived that in the street outside a car was parked that did not belong there. At my place they met the tantrica Dewi. She explained to Osiris and Honey that she was a Yajravan tantric and that her name meant Goddess of fertility. After this brief introduction Dewi gave them an explanation of Yajravan tantric. Death plays an important role in our tantric. There are two reasons for this. It helps our adherents to remember that life is impermanent. This is to keep them from getting caught up in petty concerns that mean nothing once this current incarnation is over. The other reason is that in certain tantric rituals, practioners must offer themselves up to malevolent spirits and actually let their selfhood (their ego) be killed. This extreme step is considered an important sacrifice in the quest for enlightenment. We do belief that emotions can be used to counteract and to eliminate other emotions. This is the fastest way to achieve enlightenment. Many of our practices are very emotional and very sensual. Sexual intercourse is therefore used in a ritual context to help achieve enlightenment.

Dewi and her follower Cipto started to undress. I stayed in the room. Dewi asked Honey and Osiris to undress and to copy their behavior. There the five of us were standing in the little room. Dewi explained further: Death and suffering are used in Vajravana symbolism not to encourage death and suffering but to help people to acknowledge death and suffering and to deal with it more constructively. When Yajravan Buddhist say that "life is suffering" it is not to make people suffer more, but to help them get started on the path towards suffering less. Vajravan Buddhism tries to be as open as possible about the dark side of life and the universe. They try not to mask or ignore the things which make life dangerous and full of suffering. Instead they try to explore those elements as deeply as possible to make life easier.

Dewi asked Osiris and Honey to follow her example and not to question it. She would guide them to explore their sensual feelings further. Cipto went into lotus position. Dewi went down on his thighs while his penis penetrated her. Osiris looked at me. I said it is OK. Remember who you are: you are my possession and the whore of Honey. Do as told. Osiris also took the lotus position and Honey helped him with his penetration. I put a lock through the Prince Albert piercing and the clitoris piercing. Two other locks I put through their nipple piercings. They were now chained to each other. Dewi instructed them that they had to sit in this position the whole day. During this period they had to concentrate on the seven chakras and to circulate as one unit the air through their bodies. She put her mouth on the mouth of Cipto. And they started to breath as one unit. Osiris glanced at me. I became angry and said do as I have ordered you Osiris than put his mouth on the mouth of Honey.

They started with the base chakra. When the penis of Osiris became limp Honey could slightly move or use her pelvic muscles or vaginal muscles. By using these muscles she would draw in his penis in her vagina and his phallus would become rigid again. Sometimes he lost his concentration, but then Dewi called him back on track. He was not used to the lotus position. After some time it hurts. But if you accept this pain it will gradually disappear. And so it happened. At a certain moment he lost all sense of awareness he had become once again one with Honey and the universe. But this unity was soon lost when he smelled my perfume. Concentrate again on your chakras and on the breath of you both. And after some time again the borders of his existence disappeared. At a certain moment Honey and Osiris had together a complete body orgasm. His seed was slowly sucked up into the beaver of Honey.

All at a sudden Dewi started to talk. "This is the end of the session." And she gave me a parcel. In this parcel there was a scroll with the holy secret teachings of Yajravan Buddhism. She pointed to a certain part and said to me study this part particularly well Goddess Ira since you have to use it at the end of your quest. Find the right code. She told Osiris: what you have learned today you will soon need when Goddess Ira carries out the black rite and during your stay in Mexico. Trust Goddess Ira completely you have to be completely dedicated and your ego has to fade out into her ego till the end of your days. The three of us said goodbye to Dewi and Cipto and thanked her for her invaluable lessons.

My beloved Goddess took me aside and started in different colors on the places where the seven chakras are situated to tattoo small tantric symbols. Then she did send me home.

5 Extreme. The black rite.

In the shopping mall I bought an expensive blue outfit with small stripes. This suit was made by a famous Italian fashion designer from Milan. I wanted to look my very best when I met Goddess Ira again. I wanted to impress her with my appearance.

From Goddess Ira I had received the instruction to open the gate with the lock combination 666. This gave me an uncomfortable feeling. She looked as beautiful as ever. I gave her my bouquet of forty-three red roses and 1 white rose and planted a kiss on her red lips.

She told me today and tonight will be special. "It is a day and night full of meaning and ceremony. For enlightenment it is today and tonight necessary to experience half of the wheel of Karma. These experiences are about things you don't want. But these rituals are necessary for the purification of the elect. Good and evil go together. These rituals will penetrate your core emotions and intensifies our alliance. So let me surprise you. Climb into the trunk of my car. I don't know if I will see you. "The trunk closed and the car drove away. After a while the car stopped. It took some time before the trunk was opened. When my eyes became accustomed to the darkness I saw that I was in a forest. It was foggy. In front of me there were three creatures. When I looked closely I realized that these creatures were women. The three women were dressed in black latex. The smallest one wore a latex skirt which reached to her thighs. Another girl wore a short latex pants with matching top with a large red cross in a white circle on her chest. I could see the bottom of her buttocks. Two of them were walking on high heels and the one with the red cross wore boots up to her thighs. The third one wore a latex dress which reached to her ankles. Her arms were bare. All of them wore black identical masks. These masks were made of black bird feathers with on top a feather of a peacock. Around the opening for the eyes there was gold stitching.

One of the girls made it clear by gestures that I had to get out of the car and they made it also clear to me that I had to undress. This I did. Non-verbally I was instructed to hand over my clothes and shoes. It was rather cold. My ass was freezing. There I stood in my Adam costume with my three piercings and my collar. In the distance I heard an owl.

I had to collect a basket from the car and to follow them further into the wood. After some time they stopped. I had to open the basket and to fill the glasses with champagne. There were four glasses three champagne glasses and one wine glass. I uncorked the champagne bottle and filled the four glasses. I had to fill the wine glass only a quarter and to give the full champagne glasses to the three masked ladies. The black creatures hadn't said a word. In a dark forest you hear at night all kind of scary spooky sounds which scared me a bit.

The creatures turned me around. They inserted ear plugs made of cotton into my ears. The effect was that only with great difficulty I could hear sounds. What the creatures said to each other was not possible to comprehend for me. One of them put a hood over my head. She tied it from behind. A dog collar with a heavy iron chain was fixed around my neck. After that a blinder was put over my eyes. I couldn't see and I couldn't hear anything in that dark foggy forest. It was pretty scary.

There was a pull on the chain. I had to follow. Several times I stumbled and fell while the brushwood damaged my knees. Then there was each time a pull at the chain and I had to stand-up again. After some time we stopped. Both my arms were grasped and I had to bend over. My legs were lifted. My belly came to rest on a kind of surface. I felt that my wrists, which were considerably lower than my belly, were put in cuffs which were locked. Also my knees rested on two surfaces. I got the impression that the construction had an H shape. Also my ankles were put into cuffs which were locked. My stomach was tied with a leather strap to the higher crosspiece. It was clear to me that my ass and asshole were completely exposed. They put a blanket over me. All my senses were blocked now. But then I started hearing the voices again, vaguely but then more and more clear: Osiris obeys Goddess Ira, Osiris obeys Goddess Ira, Osiris obeys Goddess Ira…

After some time when I felt almost like hypnotized by the repetition of the line:"Osiris obeys Goddess Ira", the blanket was removed. I could feel the cold of the night. Suddenly I felt a multitude of fingers and nails touch my exposed back. This went on for some time. Then nothing happened for a while, but the voice came back, first softly, then harder and faster and harder and faster, then out of the blue I felt that my buttocks were beaten with a whip. Because it was so unexpected I was not prepared. And it did hurt. The beating with the whip went on and on. I got the impression that the creatures used the whip in turn. My buttocks felt hot. It was especially painful when the lash touched from beneath and hit my penis and balls. I yelled each time and tried to escape. It was hopeless. I was angry. I felt an uncontrolled feeling of hatred and anger against these masked creatures, it felt like they flogged the images I was creating of You, my Goddess, out in a few blows, it felt like a rude awakening from a dream you would never like to end. I wanted to lash out and shout, but the chains around my wrists and ankles and the belt held me too tight. I had to think and my thoughts went to what my Goddess wanted to achieve here, as she brought me here, she must have plans for me, I have to be worthy and I have to be strong, for her. It gave me courage and I forced myself to pull myself together. I heard your voice again:"Osiris belongs to Goddess Ira, Osiris obeys Goddess Ira, and Osiris loves Goddess Ira…" It brought me back to my duty as with a snap of your finger… After they had removed the blanket, I had my three somatic senses (touch, heat / cold and pain) back. It made me remember the Dewi lecture about the path to enlightenment about our petty concerns of daily life and about the killing of our ego. She had said that emotions are a method to counteract and to eliminate other emotions. Was that the purpose? I also remembered the strange remark from Goddess Ira that I had to experience half of the wheel of Karma.

The creatures began to yell in my ears. Even through the cotton ear plugs I heard them shouting endlessly "Obey Goddess Ira". I was troubled a bit to hear these words again but by other voices each time the whip touched with full force my exposed behind or hit my balls and penis. Goddess Ira can't have prepared this for me, something got out of hand, I did not trust those women and then I couldn't bear the pain any longer. There was a feeling of hopelessness, despondency and impending doom. By now I yelled just as hard as they did. I cried: "Yes I will Obey Goddess Ira". I felt hands disappear in my anal cleft and not long after this I had to suck the fingers of the creatures.

After some time they stopped. They removed the blindfold, the hood and took the cotton ear plugs out of my ears. I could see and hear again. They put a mask made of light brown feathers on my head. I saw that there was also present a man dressed in a brown monk's cloak. He wore a brown feathered mask like mine, but in a different way. He was taking pictures and he seemed to record all that was happening.

The tallest of the creatures spoke to me. **"We are three priestesses. My name is Maxime. The identity of the two others will soon be revealed".** She was around 6 feet tall and had curling brown hair. I estimate her size at approximately 38. She possessed long shapely legs. Later I understood that she was a BDSM mistress. Her finger disappeared under her dress. With this finger she touched my nose. I had to smell it. Her finger smelled delicious. It was a mixture of her perfume and the faint smell of what can only be the personal scent of her pussy.

Close by a campfire burned. The priestess with the red cross walked over and picked something up. With this thing she walked to me. I noticed that it was a metal strap-on dildo. She also wore a similar black mask. Also Maxime went to the campfire and came back with a large black strap-on dildo. The priestess with the red cross disappeared from my sight. Suddenly I felt a sharp pain in my buttocks. It looked like a clothespin was pinned on my buttock. This was repeated three more times. Every time I cried out very loud. Later when I saw the pictures I saw that they had stuck four green feathers in my behind. Two in every buttock, the feathers were attached to long needles which were pressed through my skin. It made me anxious but at the same time the needles gave me a peaceful feeling as if they were like a familiar ritual that made me think of you. The needles were probably inserted by the smallest priestess and the priestess with the red cross.

Maxime shouted to me that the priestess with the red cross would take my virginity. While she took my virginity I had to suck her immense black cock. She had not finished her sentence when the ordeal started. Slowly the priestess with the iron strap-on dildo came closer with that thing and she touched my closing muscles with her metal dildo. My only thoughts were:"Why am I so profoundly humbled. This is a major humiliation which I cannot bear."

My muscles did initially not cooperate. My cave was closed and stayed closed. She pushed my bottom up high in the air to expose my asshole. My cave opened slowly and she boarded me. I screamed and cried and pleaded, but this dominant woman just carried on. Every time she moved her hips closer to my arse the iron dildo explored further my anus. I was taken from behind whilst I was forced to suck Maxime's cock. She said "**remember the property agreement stated that you are required to undergo any torture or humiliation and that you are not entitled to refuse anything or to stop the torture or humiliation.**" My asshole split to accommodate her. She took her time plunging in and out. I had reached my pain threshold. Did she stop? No of course not and I had to affirm that My virginity was taken away from me, by her.

Each time I wanted to stop sucking the penis of Maxime she grabbed my hair and forced me to suck her black cock. Her large cock came deeper and deeper into my mouth. Finally it disappeared completely into my throat. I hadn't expected it. I was the chosen one of Goddess Ira. I felt more important than others. Now I had to experience the opposite. I was just a toy for other women's amusement, amusement that did not give me any kind of pleasure, only pain and I felt deeply humiliated…

Meanwhile the iron cock started giving electrical shocks into my anus. The priestess with the red cross played with the current. She seemed infected by evil. Had she made a deal with the devil? The two other priestesses yelled time after time "you now belong to Goddess Ira." It became even worse. They tore with full force at the nipple piercings. They put besides the existing piercing a sharp bird feather through the existing piercing hole. This hole was too small. The blood gushed out of my right nipple and fell in big drops on the virgin forest ground. It hurt immensely. I tried to escape but to no avail. It went on and on for a long time. After some time I surrendered completely to the priestess who took me from behind, there was no energy left inside me to resist to what she was doing so my muscles released their tightness and I was entirely open for her my ego shattered. I felt not any longer ashamed and to the core humiliated but I felt I had been unfaithful to you, Goddess Ira as I had to admit that after I surrendered fully to her penetration this "rape" had become even enjoyable. Not only because by then the muscles around my anus were feeling relaxed but I had also accepted the complete dominance of an unknown woman over me. I had never surrendered myself like that in my whole life. This degree of surrendering to somebody else is only possible when ones ego is crushed. She had become one with me through the electric energy of the dildo and the constant pressure she had maintained in the in and out movement of her dildo, which seemed to be part of her, looking at the way she so naturally seemed to operate it. I felt ecstasy and the bliss of real unity. This was the black rite my Goddess had spoken about when I was in the body bag. I felt that this priestess had the uncannily ability over me to let me do things I would not do otherwise. Even those things were my natural inclination was totally opposed to. This priestess had splintered my ego just as my Goddess had promised me and she therefore could have such dominant power over me.

I felt stronger and more proud as when I entered this bizarre event. I felt proud because I had not failed and my Goddess would not be disappointed when I report to her.

Meanwhile the third priestess had moved away... I couldn't follow her with my eyes. But on the background I did hear a noise. It was the sound of liquid being poured into a glass. Then there was silence and the smallest priestess came back with two glasses, a wine glass and a champagne glass. In the wine glass, I had filled earlier, was still a little bit of champagne. She stood in front of me and poured the darker fluid from the champagne glass which she had in her left hand into the wine glass which she had in her right hand. The voice of the priestess behind me said, "You will now drink the virgin nectar of my only daughter."

I was stunned because only then I recognized your voice and understood that the virgin priestess was the witness Charlotte. It was you who had penetrated me and to whom I had surrendered completely, how I could have missed the lovely perfume I suddenly smelled. I felt even more proud that you, my Goddess had actually, not only witnessed, but physically seen and felt my physical and emotional surrender. It could not have been anyone else; I realized then, because who would have the strength and the knowledge of how to make me submit this way. I had not been unfaithful to you.

You then removed the chains from my wrists so I could now move a little bit backwards. You pulled my head back and I had to open my mouth while the virgin priestess poured her liquid into my mouth. It was still hot and it tasted rather well. I was glad that it was your daughter's nectar, and I saw it as it was intended, a gift from the Goddesses, virgin Champaign as a reward for the pain and pain levels I came to overcome. Then it dawned on me that I'd got my five senses back those which I had lost earlier.

The cuffs around my ankles and the leather belt were unlocked by the three of you. I was free and could stand-up straight; I stretched my muscles a bit but then. With the chain still around my neck you, my Goddess brought me to the campfire. There you ordered me to lie on the floor. My arms and legs were then fixed onto large tent hooks. You and Maxime faced each other and with a single nod Maxime moved to the middle part of my body and parked her shoe on my lower belly, not pushing, just resting and then you, my Goddess did the same but alongside my head and then you placed your boot on my mouth. I was no longer in fear because I was one with you and I trusted you completely. You winked at Maxime and you both stood high above me, I could feel Maximes ankles on each side of my lower body and I could feel your latex boots pressing against my right and left shoulder. As in a very well synchronized ballet, you both pushed aside your panties. In the flames of the nearby campfire I had a good view of your smoothly shaven pussies. You ordered me to open my mouth and I received your champagne into my mouth while I received Maxime's golden shower simultaneously over my penis and the whole of my pubic area. They felt like hot showers. The undiluted golden shower of you my Goddess tasted very different from the virgin nectar mixed with champagne from your daughter, the young priestess. The young priestess and you my Goddess had released your nectar into my mouth and I had recaptured your life forces from your sources. I thanked both of you for your gift. You ordered me to lie like this for awhile so that your fluids could be well absorbed into my skin. Then both the other priestesses washed my body with a liquid that smelled like papaya and coffee and then rubbed me dry with a towel.

Then they brought me back to you, blindfolded and I had to kneel before you, head down and my arms above my head, they folded my hands into a position that felt like I was offering you something, but I could not see and I was too taken by the amazing powers you had over me that I assumed the best thing to do was to let the three of you guide me, I would simply follow, and follow your orders, without even thinking about it, to OBEY … that's what you were all whispering, shouting, what I imagined or dreamed or made up, but it was true, I was here and I was nothing but obeying…to you, Goddess Ira.

You lifted up my head but held my hands with a firm grip of your hand in the same offering position whilst the other hand pulled the blindfold off … I was facing you whilst you reached beside you to pick up a shiny object. When it came closer and in my field of view I saw it was a small silver sharp knife and you used it to make a small incision between your right thumb and index finger. You moved your hand closer to my face where I could see the bubble of blood the cut had caused, you then pushed it towards your lips and ordered me to open my mouth only slightly, your hand touched my tong and you ordered me to suck and swallow it. You had made me drink your blood and declared solemnly "by drinking my blood and my urine you carry a part of me in you. Your health will be influenced by my health and My illness will now be your illness." I had to drink your blood till the wound stopped bleeding. By drinking your blood we had now established a blood relationship between us a kind of kinship that existed also between Osiris, Isis and Horus.

I had given my blood to Osiris. He had received a part of my human soul my Ib or metaphysical heart the seat of my emotion, my thought, my will and my intention. Now all of this had to grow inside Osiris.

I was then invited to sit in the middle of a triangle formed by the three priestesses. Charlotte was sitting behind me. My body rested comfortably against her body. She felt very soft and warm. Maxim sat on her knees at the left and you were seated at my right side. You ordered me to masturbate. I was enclosed on both sides and my back by your warm bodies in the dark forest whilst I was masturbating. Too soon my seed flowed out of my penis into a wooden cup that was placed between my knees, you took it and added a powder to it and some mineral water and said: "your seed you need to eat!" I obeyed, again without asking myself any questions as to the why and the how … You then told me I could put on my raincoat and shoes. I had to describe what had happened today in a poem, especially written for you, my Goddess

Afterwards we talked a bit. The conversation was most of the time focused on the seven deadly sins and the seven virtues that weave our wheel of Karma. You repeated your earlier remark that today and tonight we had only focused on half of the wheel of Karma. You started explaining

"When you arrived here today you were overdressed. At that time you expressed the sins of extravagance (**Luxuria**) and greed (**Avaritia**). To behave like that you were disloyal to my spiritual teachings and guided by your own vanity to cure you from these sins you had to undress in front of us. You will lose your beautiful suit and it must have been clear to you by now that greed doesn't bode well. Now I throw your beautiful suite into the flames of the campfire. The flames flirted with the Italian fabric while the fire flared up. But the sin of luxuria also includes lust or lechery; those are excessive thoughts and or desires of a sexual nature.

You went on; "When you were whipped I saw an uncontrollable feeling of hatred and anger towards us. At that time you committed the deadly sin of wrath (**Ira**).When you subsequently gave in it was because you felt hopeless. This is the deadly sin of discouragement (**Acedia**). You must understand as long as there is life you may never give up.

When you had to suck the big black cock of Maxime and were taken by me from behind this was done to learn you that pride (**Superbia**) is the ultimate source from which the other deadly sins arise. When you had to gulp down our nectar you committed the sin of gluttony (**Gula**).You are also sometimes jealous. I feel that. I know that you would prefer to have sex with me. You envy those who have it and want to deprive them of it. Also this is a deadly sin (**Invidia**). Maybe you now better understand the words of Dewi when she spoke about their practices. Practices that are very emotional and sensual. Practices which are all directed to spiritual enlightenment. A state were duality doesn't exist. The wheel of Karma has two opposite sides. Good and evil go together.

Opposite the seven deathly sins are the seven virtues: chastity (Castitas), temperance (Temperantia), charity (Caritas), diligence (Industria), patience (Patientia) and kindness (Humanitas).

I do hope that through the experience of today and tonight you will understand the wheel of Karma much better. This is necessary because you have to be spiritually, mentally and bodily cleaned in order to be the chosen one. Only with the chosen one I can fulfill my calling and save the world. For further purification and to fulfill my quest you have to travel to Japan, Egypt and to Mexico. It will be dangerous and difficult. After this you will understand that everything is impermanent and will change. You will then also understand that life without suffering is impossible and if you think you can avoid it you will suffer more pain. You also will understand that nothing has an immutable core.

By making a public display of Osiris subjugation in front of the others his self-image became even more soft and prepared for the final blows. It was like a game of chess. First I had to break down his identity as a man and when that goal had been reached his identity finally could coincide with my identity. As part of this game of chess I told him I had invited a woman and a man with whom I expected him to have intercourse... Why did I play with his mind like this? I knew he had a strong aversion towards homosexual acts. He would have done anything to avoid it. So I told him he had a week to mentally prepare for this as I did not accept an excuse or cancellation, unless followed by a very severe punishment... He looked at me and in my eyes I am sure he must have picked up that I meant business. So he promised me he would be ready for this humiliating event and would not disappoint me then he mumbled something like that he would focus on the woman and keep his eyes closed to picture me with a strapon–on in front of him or behind him, as he had no idea if I was going that far as to have another man humiliate his freshly lost virginity arse.

I decided to punish him for his mumbling as it is a bit disrespectful and said that he had to present himself with a clean and shaven arsehole.

I can imagine the horror scenarios that were displayed in his brain but at the date and the time we agreed on Osiris presented himself with a smile and forty-three white roses and one red one.

I told him that I had decided to postpone part 2 as he needed more time

Goddess Ira and Osiris

to accurately place the events from last week, as I had noticed in his writings and reports, which I all had to delete, that he hadn't come to a consensus .

I could see his eyes flickering of joy, but his mouth said;"O that's a pity, I was almost looking forward to it." Of course I told him off for bluffing and explained that I, in theory would have to replace one ordeal with another because of him mocking me, pretending to be eager instead of courageous, I could tell Osiris felt very relieved. And by believing it was postponed to a later date and to be happy with this postponement he was actually choosing to engage in a more identity destroying behavior. This would be my fifth and final step in the destruction of the identity of Osiris.

When he left I requested him to put on the chastity device. If he did this he would erode his masculinity further. I told him that in the BDSM community it is called "castration". I told him that I would be very happy if he voluntary "castrated" himself because by this act he was showing how much he cared for me. Of course he had no problem to put on the chastity device for me, it was a pleasure. By voluntary giving up the sexual freedom of his dick he had renounced an important part of his identity. This "castration" was an intermediate step that was necessary for the final blow to his manhood which I had mapped on the vision board in my kitchen. Since his clothes were taken away he was only wearing his raincoat, chastity device and shoes. I gave him a kiss and send him home.

When he got home I reminded him about what I had said about lust or lechery as part of the deathly sin Luxuria. I told him we need to explore this issue a little bit further. "I have decided upon a ritual context in which I want you to have sexual intercourse with our guests. Prepare yourself for this event. "

That was all I wrote in the mail, I gave him 14 days, which I knew he would suffer from not being able to see me sooner, but I wanted the pain of missing me to out measure the dislike for the event that I had forced upon him.

The day finally arrived. It would be a special event and it would last the whole evening. Goddess Ira told me there would be in total seven people. One woman and four men she had invited and then me and herself. She told me it had to be mystical, anonymous but exciting she referred to a movie called EYES WIDE SHUT where Everyone would be dressed with black capes and feathered masks on. She said the intention was that, I, Osiris would be invited on to a black bed where a masked woman would be already displayed, yet covered by her black cape, and one high heeled person would

The Elevation to Divinity

be alongside the bed standing, also wearing the cape and another feathered mask.

You then told me to take a shower and dress into the cape with red lining inside you had ordered me to bring. I knew she had said I had to have intercourse with a woman and her partner. The person alongside the bed was wearing high heels so she might have been teasing me about the men all along.

When I heard the showerhead had gone silent I went to the bathroom to fetch Osiris and brief him again about the ritual I had planned for him, stage 2 of the black rite. I placed the feathered mask over his eyes and clicked my lead onto his slavecollar, he shivered for a minute and I smiled, as this was going to give me joy…

I brought him to the bed and introduced him to the woman, ordering him to gently stroke her and then kiss her in the neck, stroke her breasts and feel her warm lips that she had already displayed eager and open and had been, as I had asked her before, busy with herself getting herself in the right kind of mood… I know these things are not that obvious, straight from the office to a sexfest.

The woman was a horny woman I had met before; it was that horny behavior of hers that made me choose them to be the ones that would give Osiris his first encounter with a threesome. Of course I knew that Osiris thought all that was required of him was a few minutes of cocksuck whilst the woman would be sucking him at the same time and I had picked up from his relaxed behavior that the high heeled boots probably gave him the impression I had hoped for. He thought it to be his lucky day and he would have a sexfest with two women.

I turned back to the acts I had ordered Osiris to perform and was surprised that they were merely lying next to each other without any real drive … it made me raise my voice and I snapped at Osiris that he was not here to bore the woman to sleep and that I expected more action and engagement from him. I had to call him to the order again 3 times after again and I saw that the woman was feeling quite bored. Also the person alongside did not get turned on by the weak performance of the two players who obviously could not find the yin and the yan with each other.

I had told Osiris that she was a horny woman and that the other men would probably be no more than spectators. I knew Osiris had no desire at all to participate in this event. Sex with a woman even his wife was difficult enough for him. He loved and adored me his Goddess, although that is not a physical vanilla love. But I knew he had no appetite at all to have sex with a man. The prospect had given him many sleepless nights. But he knew he had to obey his Goddess and respect her wishes. I knew Osiris needed a bit of extra stimulation as he kept looking for me and signaling me to come closer, of course that was not part of the arrangement, I had no intention to go and hold hands …so I ordered him to stand-up and I gave him a small towel impregnated with my perfume and ordered him to smell it and inhale it very deeply.

Then I heard voices downstairs and texted my friend to entertain the guests until it was time for them to come up. To my surprise I noticed that Osiris had grown hard and big, much to the woman's liking, I could tell, so I told Osiris to lick the woman, on the breasts, under the armpits and then on her clit by pulling her legs apart and sucking and licking the clit, I had to correct his movements and position a bit and advised the woman that she can grab hold of his head and push him into a rhythm she preferred… then she pushed him up and she sucked his cock at the same time, as Osiris got quickly very hard (I wondered if it was a natural excitement or that it was mainly my voice coming out of my rc hypno which unconsciously brought him back to think about his Goddess and his mission and what she required of him) I ordered him to change his position and brought him seated on his knees and buried his face between her thighs, that position was the trigger for the second person present to join in with the ritual.

Whilst Osiris face was enclosed between the woman's legs and she enclosed it firmly, Osiris was in a vulnerable position with his backside.

The other person present was the bi-sexual crossdressing husband of the woman and I had agreed on the actions he had to take to let Osiris overcame his adversity to the male population in the bedroom or connected to it …So the crossdresser sat next to the bed and had Osiris arse within reach, I winked him to wait and I gave Osiris a few slaps on his butt to let him know I was there, and he was held firmly by a pair of legs so could not escape from that place.

I heard the woman have her first orgasm and I heard Osiris swallow her juices, at that point the crossdresser started caressing Osiris arse (he must have thought it was me perhaps) Osiris did not object, then the crossdresser started rimming Osiris's arse and I don't think Osiris minded that at all, au contraire, he lifted his arse higher and higher and the crossdresser started going in deeper and fucked his arse with his tongue.

I told Osiris he had to continue giving the woman pleasure until further orders.

The Elevation to Divinity

Then I summoned the first visitor up... He took his place alongside the bed and was dressed like all the others, black cape and feathered mask.

I told Osiris that it was now time to penetrate the woman and I winked at the woman to take care of the condom. Osiris went inside her and the crossdresser followed him, having his own sex on display now for the new guest, who I ordered to go down on his knees and suck the crossdresser...,

Then I summoned the second guest up. He took his place behind the bed... I told him to kneel over the woman's head and told the woman that she had a second cock at her disposal, she started licking the cock whilst Osiris was still fucking her and being caressed in his arse by the crossdresser who was being held hard by the other guest. Then I ordered Osiris to do the same as the woman had done to the hard cock that was in front of his face. He obeyed and first touched as if he was scared of the thing, but then when I repeated:"Osiris obeys Goddess Ira "several times, he took the cock in his mouth.

I summoned guest number three up and he presented his cock to the woman.

As the bed and its surroundings became very crowded I told Osiris that he could give the cock to the woman who had then two cocks to suck and that he had to fuck her hard now whilst the crossdresser had put two fingers up his arse.

He was going in high tempo and shouted that he could not hold it much longer... so I ordered him to let it all float and he came very long and intense, due to the built up and excitement.

I then told the crossdresser and the man who was giving him head that they could take Osiris' place and I took Osiris to the bathroom and ordered him to have his shower and meet me downstairs after.

To the other people and guest number four who was waiting outside the door, I said that they had the place to themselves and that they could go on and enjoy themselves.

It had been one of the wishes of the woman: she would only come if she would know there were lots of cocks to fuck and suck as she wanted a good ride.

Well I was sure that that would not be a problem as I had invited four real stallions to help her achieve that pleasure.

I went downstairs and waited for Osiris.

When he came down he looked a bit troubled and I asked him how he felt after this part of forced bisexuality. He said he had mixed feelings and that he had to focus on his mission and my voice to bring it to a good end.

He handed me the condom with his sperm and I put it in the freezer. I told him we would come back to this in a later stage.

I gave him an espresso coffee and he smoked a cigar, whilst I had a glass of alter ego from margaux, one of my favorite red wines. I told him I was pleased about the evening and said he had performed well. He had now overcome another fear and he had learned to make the best of this degrading situation I had put him in.

I told him I wanted a report, as usual, about only "the feelings and doubts" during the whole process, I did not want any details about anything else...

I told him to kneel in front of me and pushed his head to my boots and said he had to kiss them and thank me for the new experience and overcome fear.

He repeated what I told him and then I told him he could get up and make his way home.

I gave him a big hug and a kiss on his forehead and said to him: "this was the first part, there is more to come!"

Then I closed the door behind him and I knew he would think about what I could have meant with those words. I saw myself smile when I passed by the mirror.

When I went into the car, I was still deep in my subspace. Although I physically drove away most of me that was left of me stayed behind. I was confused, depressed and proud. Actually I couldn't handle the situation at all. Was this what I wanted and was I the right person for my Goddess during her quest. I doubted and doubted. Again and again I replayed over and over in my mind what had happened. Yes ultimately I had liked the rimming and I also had enjoyed even more the beaver and the juices of the horney woman. But most of all I had liked the fact that my Goddess was present and was proud of me. I had smelled her deliciously sent. And during some time I had thought she was with me. That it was my Goddess who was caressing my behind. But now it was clear for me that she had not participated. My Goddess had made me a bisexual. I couldn't any longer deny that. And because my Goddess had done that it made me in a strange way very proud. I had done it for her. I had scarified my manhood for her. I had not failed her. I had focused on her mission and her voice. It was clear that my norms and values were changing.

During the two weeks that followed I was proud but most of the time depressed and confused. When my depression was very bad and it looked that I couldn't handle the situation any longer I solved my problem by looking at her pictures and by hearing her voice. That was the only way I filled the void of my in time and place lingering subspace. During that awful time I would have given anything for a hug and a kiss from her.

Although I am a very dedicated and loyal person I am sure in retrospect that this would have been insufficient to continue my relationship with my Goddess. However it was the strong and indestructible anchor of my love for my Goddess, my believe and trust in her and our property agreement what made me persist. I could not resist the invitation to meet her two weeks later. On the contrary I counted the days, the hours, the minutes and seconds. But the clock would hardly move. All the time I was thinking about what did she mend with her closing remark. "There is more to come". Finally the clock surrendered and it was time to meet her again.

Two weeks had passed and I had sent Osiris the new entrance code to the gate. He wrote me he would arrive in 5 minutes.

Exactly 5 minutes later I saw him in.

This time he had a bouquet of forty-four pink roses and one red rose for me. He also gave me the promised poem. The poem is put into two black frames. The color of the frames is black because of the black rite. At the top of the first frame is the black mask of me Goddess Ira. The peacock feather protrudes above the frame. This was done as he explained because I am the light of the world and his guide. The second black frame has at the bottom Osiris brown mask. The position of the masks represents the relation between Top and Bottom. On both side of the poem little pictures of the participants in the black rite were printed. I Goddess Ira put the frames on top of the fireplace. This is his poem.

Extreme Emotional

A 666 lock
To mock
My purification
A Bottoms inclination
Three black feathered priestesses with a peacock on top
One is my Top
Fixed with a chain
To ordain
Senses blocked
By three priestess alternately flogged
Flared emotions

Unearthly passions
Me obeying the Goddess
In total blackness
Completely altered
My ego splintered
My senses returned
My soul yearned
A courtesan veil of brown plumage
Green feathers as ass camouflage
A cock in my throat
And a gloat
The red cross took my virginity
Done brusquely by my infinity
She is my captor
She is my ego's annihilator
The holy hot water of the virgin
A taste so elfin
Panties pushed aside
Legs over my head astride
In my purview
Who you screw
Sacred deluge of hot pee
From Maxime and my Queen Bee
Drinking the Goddess blood
I received my pureblood
My seed freed
I concede
My Goddess procreation
Is my ego's castration

Osiris

I had to continue the chess game. I asked Osiris to leave the room and I found an address on the computer. I told Osiris that we had to go outside. We got into the car and parked the car close by our red light district. Osiris didn't know this. I put him a blindfold on and walked with him to the red lights. It was raining cats and dogs. But nevertheless there were many horny men on the street looking into the windows if they could find a woman of their taste. Obviously the man in the street and the women in the windows found it weird the way I walked with Osiris. I deliberately walked the streets a few times back and forth. Finally Osiris and I entered one of the buildings. We were brought to a sparsely lit small room.

There I met the Shemale Vicky. She looked attractive. I did choose an attractive Shemale on purpose to make it a little bit easier for Osiris to cross the threshold. If he crossed this threshold his identity as a man would be forever changed. An attractive Shemale would facilitate Osiris identity reframing. I hoped that I had prepared him well because if I had prepared him well Vicky would give Osiris manhood an unrecoverable powerful blow. Osiris compliance was important for the reframing of his (sexual) identity.

Vicky had completely shaved her body and was 5.93 feet tall. Vicky had long black hair and brown eyes. Her skin was dark brown and she came from Chile. Osiris had still his blindfold on. I paid Vicky and gave Osiris the command to undress. Then I took his blindfold off. I could see that he was shocked. I saw in his eyes a last-minute resistance. Would he comply? To overcome his resistance I promised him to be present and to encourage him but I also wanted to be sure that he did what he had to do. I told him that in Vicky he had the combination of man and woman in 1 form, as he had completed the previous task of sex with a woman and a man, this had to be his second step to have sex with both in one.

I gave him the order to lie on the bed and to cares and to kiss her. After a little encouragement from me he concurred with my request. He accepted the fondling silently of Vicky this was a sign for me that his identity reframing was occurring. The bra had to stay on but Osiris had to take of her skirt. Under the skirt she wore a white string. This Osiris had to remove as well. We saw a particularly long and sturdy cock without pubic hair. Osiris was completely surprised because he has no small Willie but this one was from a different category almost alien. I give him the choice to offer oral service to Vicky a service he already had experienced with Maxime, Honey and with the black caped visitor or to fuck her.

I knew of course in advance his choice. After some time he put the penis of Vicky in his hands. He hesitated but finally he did it. He put the huge cock in his mouth. Meanwhile Vicky had Osiris pick in her mouth and began enthusiastically to work on it. At the start Osiris did not do so well. It disappointed me so I told him and then I encouraged him because I knew he could do a lot better He had to mimic Vicky with the fellatio. After some time I put my hands on Osiris head and moved his head down on the penis of Vicky. The dick of Vicky came deeper and deeper into his mouth.

Goddess Ira and Osiris

Rhythmically the hard cock of Vicky went up and down into his mouth and throat. I got the impression that Osiris finally enjoyed it a little bit.

After some while I asked Osiris to fuck her in her arse. This he did immediately without comments. This was important information for me because I now knew for sure that he had voluntary given up his manhood. With hard shoves he fucked her. But he couldn't come. Then it was the turn of Vicky. After this Osiris put again her pick in his mouth. This time I didn't assist Osiris. Vicky ejaculated in the mouth of Osiris. Osiris lost his erection again so I started repeating "Osiris obeys Goddess Ira" and that seemed to work, his penis became hard and Finally Osiris fucked her again in her arse. I encouraged him again by repeating over and over again "Osiris obeys Goddess Ira". This gave the desired result. He ejaculated in her arse. I ordered him to put a knot in the condom and to take it home. This condom with his seed is now as a trophy in my freezer. A trophy which represents the giving up of his (sexual) identity for me. I had succeeded in the destruction of the identity of Osiris. I will cherish this trophy as long as I life. After saying goodbye to Vicky we left in the pouring rain and went home.

After these extreme events, I, the Bottom of you Goddess Ira, needed you more than ever. I was very emotional. I had even more than usually a need for this connection with you and for your hugs. I enjoyed it when I was allowed to entangle with you on the couch at your home and to smell your fragrance. For me this was the only way back out of the extreme subspace you had created for me. My energy had to come in balance again. My body and mind had to recover from all what I endured.

When I first met Osiris I started to reframe in steps his identity. I had on the vision board five major steps designed. First he had to be connected for ever with me. This I did by branding him. Secondly he had to become my property. Thirdly I had to mentally subjugate him to me. Fourthly I had to teach him that he had to subjugate to the woman and to focus only on me. The fifth step was now also a major success. An important component of Osiris self-image was his sexual identity. I had to lead him to a point of no return. This involved that he did things that were not compatible with his manhood. His manhood had to be shattered to be able to create a new self-image my image. I had shattered his manhood today. I had him where I wanted him. He had agreed to voluntary sodomy. A complete sexual identity inversion had taken place. That he ejaculated was also important because it meant that his identity was permanently reframed. He had engaged for me his beloved Goddess voluntary into sodomy. I had emasculated him. It seemed that Osiris shame and jealousy had completely disappeared and was replaced with complete trust, profound love and unshakable admiration for me. My norms and my values had become his norms and his values...

On the solid basis of the now "castrated" Osiris I could build my identity inside him. I could make my Egyptian soul perfect. Osiris already had received my name (Ren) and my blood (Ib). From then on I could predominantly concentrate on the three remaining elements of my Egyptian soul. Osiris had to acquire my personality (Sheut) and spiritual essence (Ka). He had to be unique (Ba) in the same way as I am. His identity had to coincide fully with mine identity. I was confident that I could succeed because I had created a void which had to be filled and Osiris loved me.

I said to Osiris: "Experiences are packed. But if an experience is not pleasant we usually don't grab it. Too bad, because then you may miss the hidden message. That was precisely the lesson that you needed. That is why we did do all these things. The hidden message was that your identity had to be smashed completely and that it has to fade ultimately into my identity. You must become my Egyptian soul. There is no room left for "you". The "you" has now disappeared but now you have mentally and spiritually to coincide with me. You have to cede your "penis". You know as well as I do that this is needed for the fulfillment of my quest.

I could see the love for me in Osiris eyes shining like precious diamonds. I know that he is happy when I am around and that all borders between him and me are starting to disappear. I was sure of his love and obedience. But the chess play with Osiris was not over yet.

Now it was time to build his new identity. When Osiris went to his home I put him a chastity belt on. In this chastity belt was a body worn receiver which belonged to a small remote control device. It is a male management training system which recently had come on the market. This male management system allowed me to make my own rules and to customize it to my needs. I gave him the USB interface. This allowed me to control Osiris even better remotely. It is an effective device which learned him my preferences and tastes by heart and to behave and to exceed to my expectations. Positive punishment and negative reinforcement automatically pruned his bad habits from his brain at the touch of my button. It made altering his behavior patterns inescapable.

I shared daily my feelings and thoughts with Osiris. Osiris was obligated to write them down and to repeat them continuously till they became part of him. If e.g. if I said I think this or that he had to write down "I think this or that" or if I told him I feel dominant he had to write down "I feel dominant". The I form made it easier to make my thoughts and feelings his. The hardest part was not the writing down that was just a tool but he also had to think or feel it really. I instructed him also that every waking hour he had to imagine that he was inside my body and to feel how my body felt and to think the way I think. He had to estrange from his own body and to ascent in my body. The management training system was helpful in changing Osiris.

Regularly I called him or send him an email to check about his progress. Then I asked Osiris what do you think and feel about this or that. If the answer deviated from what I thought or felt I punished him with the small remote control device. I quite often doubted if I would succeed. My feelings were the most difficult for Osiris to grab. When something happened with me he had to feel the same way as I felt. But in the end I succeeded more and more. His penis had become superfluous. Although there were doubts ultimately I believed in my divine powers and I knew that I would save the world and that Osiris would be ready as my Egyptian soul to interflow with me in Mexico. But Mexico would be the last step of Osiris reframing.

However I still had to test Osiris and his submission towards woman and his submission towards me on a larger public ground.

I decided to create an avatar for him on a BDSM networking site.

Through this platform he could have easy access to find out even more about his Goddess by watching her pictures and movies and the comments of her to others and the other way around.

I wanted to introduce him to some of my friends there and let him become friends with them.

This was a test to check how submissive he would address my female friends and how he would describe his role in my life… and yes when I told him to contact Mistress Lauretta he already made his first mistake.

Of course he did not know that I had already informed mistress Lauretta about him and what I expected from him as my owned one.

She immediately told him off and reported to me that, also in her eyes, his submission was still partly filled with shame and the ego was broken in my presence and where I was included but when I was not present he still wanted to hide his submissive side as it was overshadowed by his own male ego.

Mistress Lauretta is a very beautiful and attractive Dominatrix from Holland and a good friend of mine. She is also very skilled and very well equipped with the right kind of toys to play with her submissives … but she has another very good skill… She is a hypnotherapist and has been for a number of years, very qualified and very experienced.

In my talks with Mistress Lauretta we decided that we would invite Osiris to her house with me arriving there a bit later and she would work on him under hypnoses to create a submissive platform in his subconscious. His submission towards other women and his complete submissive role towards his Goddess had to be put into his subconscious so that the conscious would not make mistakes as described before, again.

I called Osiris and told him to take a free afternoon the next Thursday and I would meet him at her place at 2 pm …

Due to the distance it is away from where I reside I arrived fifteen mins later and I was pleased to find Osiris naked on his knees, waiting for me. I smiled at Mistress Lauretta and she replied: "I knew this was the way you wanted him to wait for you! The last thing I wanted was a nervous sub asking me every 5 minutes if his Goddess has arrived yet!" It made me laugh out loud and I congratulated her on her actions.

Osiris then had to kiss my boots as a sign of welcome. After that he wanted to get up with the excuse that he had a present for his Goddess, but I told him very cold that this could wait and he was not allowed up until I ordered him so.

So he resumed his position on his knees on the floor.

I had a male friend with me as an extra challenge for Osiris to be openly the most submissive of all of us, in that I made him overcome his shame for his submissive nature towards men, certainly men that move in kink circles (smile)

After a bit of catching up on gossip and news on both sides we decided that the hypnosis could start.

Mistress Lauretta was dressed in leather with rubber and very high heels, she looked amazing and her heels on the wooden floor were like music to slave's ears…

Her corset was pulled in tight and you could see how tiny her waist was…She has a very good figure, I noticed and I am sure that Osiris must have been impressed to.

We decided that it would be best to have Osiris on the bench, like in any other doctor's cabinet.

Mistress Lauretta started talking to Osiris about a point somewhere on the ceiling, she told him to find the spot and to keep staring at it "never let go of the spot, it will become your spot, don't take your eyes away from it as you don't want to lose your spot, keep staring. you will see that your spot will start moving slowly, bouncing a bit, keep your eyes on your spot, follow its movements."

I was carefully following Osiris movements and he did exactly as mistress Lauretta ordered him, he stared at an invisible spot on the ceiling and he did not want to take his eyes away from it… It seemed to me that the trance had already started.

Then mistress Lauretta told him "your eyes want to keep following the spot, but it becomes harder and harder, your eyes are getting tired and your eyelids very heavy, you feel like you want to fall asleep, but I tell you, you must not, keep these eyes open and don't close them, as soon as you give in to it you will fall asleep and we don't want this yet…"

I could see that he was flickering with his eyes struggling to keep them open…

Mistress Lauretta continued: "your eyes are now so heavy it's almost impossible to keep them open, although you keep trying but there will be a point when it's no longer possible and you will fall asleep, it will be the only thing you want to do, that's to close your eyes and fall asleep…"

Osiris tried to keep them open less than a minute and then had to give in to closing them … he was now under hypnoses.

Mistress Lauretta confirmed to me that he was under hypnoses and explained a bit what she intended to do and I repeated to her what the goal was I wanted to achieve … Osiris submissive feelings had to be made stronger and colored with pride instead of shame towards others and his submission towards women had to be achieved by just a snap of my fingers ..

I filled Mistress Lauretta in on the device I already had been using on Osiris as mind control and explained that I wanted to be able to remove this whenever I saw him ready to fulfill his mission without any help of electronics. She confirmed that working on his subconscious would be a way or a help to achieve this when removing the electronic device.

I also explained her what had happened on previous occasions where my voice helped him to achieve the goals I had set for him.

I could see she was intrigued and smiled in an accomplish way.

She then turned back to Osiris and started talking "Your Goddess Ira, who is present here, your gorgeous Goddess Ira, who you are lucky to serve has confided in me that she is not happy in the way you portray yourself as her submissive to others and looking back on the mail you have sent me I can only agree with her, Your Goddess asked me to make you aware that this has to change and that your ego also has to be broken in your subconscious. That's why we are here now … we will make a journey through your subconscious and we will correct some of the triggers there…

The Elevation to Divinity

you will be included and submitted to an interview that will tell me how honest and true you are to your Goddess and to yourself."

I saw that Osiris stayed very still until Mistress Lauretta told him:

"I will ask you some questions and you will answer with a simple YES or NO, you will choose something on your body as a device to talk to me "

She gave him a few examples like lifting up right hand for YES, left for NO, raising a finger or nodding, a foot movement…

Then she asked him: "Is your beloved Goddess present here?"

It took at least a minute before we could see a tiny little movement of his right hand.

"Was your Goddess already here when you arrived?"

A little more clearly we could see his pointing finger on his left hand go up.

"Did your Goddess arrive here hours later? "

Again the finger of his left hand.

"Do you adore your Goddess?"

The finger of his right hand.

"Are you true to your Goddess?"

The finger of his right hand

"Have you ever lied to your Goddess?

The finger of his left hand

"Have you ever withheld information from your beloved Goddess and in that way also betrayed her in withholding this information "

The finger of his right hand, which meant that Osiris was not and had not been honest with me about certain events or feelings, interesting…

"Do you fantasize about your Goddess in a way the Goddess has forbidden you to do so? "

The finger of his right hand again.

"Will you come clear about this to your Goddess?"

Right finger.

"Will you tell her now, or at the end of the session?

Left finger

"Will you tell her later, when you are alone with your Goddess? "

Right finger.

I felt that this was already an important piece of information. I could only think what it could be as that he was not being honest about the fantasies he has for the nature of our relationship. I will talk to him about that on his next visit.

Then Mistress Lauretta explained why she had used this kind of technique to bring him under hypnoses, it was to make us able to follow every bit of it and to be reassured it was real, she said:" I will give you another example to reassure you how deep he is under, I will tell him to cross his arms over his chest and he won't be able to escape from this position, his arms will feel like they are glued into each other and on his chest "

Osiris was then told to try and free himself out of this position but he could not. Mistress Lauretta said I could try it for myself and yes, there was no way I could pull his arms away from each other. He was definitely deep under.

She then continued working on his mind and started telling him a story about him being in front of a lake with shiny silver water where he could see his reflection in. She asked him if he could see his reflection and informed Osiris that from now on he was able to use his voice for giving answers. She told him to describe what he saw. He described the lake as he saw it and the reflection of himself staring in the water. He was dressed and had a coat over his shoulder. She then told him to move away from the water and to follow the path that led him into a field of yellow flowers, she told him how heavy his coat had become and how much he wanted to leave this behind until he finally did.

He crossed a few more fields in different colors, which all represented a certain emotional state, until he reached the mountain top where he could meet up with his beloved Goddess.

He was naked in front of her as he could not face her any other way, it was as if he had left everything he was behind in his climb up that mountain and there his unconscious was taken into the care of his Goddess... he felt relieved and safe and did not want to feel any different for the rest of his life. His all being belonged to his Goddess now.

I listened with attention to the very nice and colorful story mistress Lauretta was telling and the responses of Osiris, describing in detail what this meant for his being.

It was clear that he could not be inventing this and Mistress Lauretta smiled at me to confirm that the session here was a success.

She then said to Osiris that his ego now belonged to goddess Ira and she asked him to describe his way back from the mountain, through the fields of flowers and how he found his left behind belongings back on his path, but all of them were so much lighter until he arrived back in front of the silver shining lake.

She then said: "Osiris move closer to the edge of the water and bend over to see your reflection again and tell me what you see?"

"I see myself… with green eyes "

This meant that his unconscious had given up his ego to become one with his Goddess on a non-conscious level.

Victory is what I thought and I nodded at Mistress Lauretta with approval.

She then said to me: "Shall we test his submission and his shame for it now? There should be a change at least some we can find?"

She continued… "Goddess Ira, you can interact with your Osiris now and give him orders and he will hear you … "She then said the same to Osiris as in that he could hear the voice of his Goddess now.

I told him to get up and go on hands and feet in front of me, he had to listen to my voice to know where I was, his eyes were open but not present.

He got on hands and feet as I had wrongly said as I wanted to say hands and knees.

Mistress Lauretta told me that orders are always followed by the letter and hands and feet are a different position than hands and knees. A bit like talking to an autist.

I knew a lot about that from the past and so I corrected myself.

I gave Osiris a few orders in positioning himself and some orders to humiliate himself in front of us.

When he was in a position on his back with one hand pulling hard on his testicles and one hand three fingers up his arse, mistress Lauretta asked me if it was ok if she woke him up like this to make him see what he was doing.

Of course I agreed…

She then said: "Osiris, you will be able to open your eyes again and you will be able to see what you are doing, however you will not be able to change anything from the position your Goddess choose to put you in, your fingers will be glued to your body. I tell you "now" and you will open your eyes and you watch …"now" "

Osiris opened his eyes and saw what he was doing, surprised about how flexible he had rolled into this position but without any sense of shame. He could not move his hands or arms and when I tried pulling they felt like glued into his body.

Mistress Lauretta asked if she could put him back to sleep and I said she could of course.

We then talked about options and possibilities of what we could achieve this way and decided that we would seriously consider doing more sessions like these in future also to other people.

Mistress Lauretta told me that she did not mix her being a pro Domme with being a pro hypnotherapist in sessions before because of ethic reasons because she is a qualified person.

I told her I believed in what I saw and with enough care and knowing the person you submit to this with mutual consent there was a probably still quite new field open for us to discover, we could simulate pain for real painsluts who can't go home with marks, we could create bisexual actions amongst slaves without the actual risks of Somas, we could submit people deeper or correct the balance between submission and obsession…

There were so many possibilities.

Mistress Lauretta then told me that a person under hypnosis will be able to take more do more and allow more in this state but will never act beyond his limits. So she gave as example that Osiris will not kill or hurt when we tell him to as it is not in the nature of his being.

But I said I wanted to try if we could make him "take" more… I had been staring at the wonderful collection of canes in Mistress Lauretta's studio and said I want to see if he will be able to handle my cane strokes now in this state as he cant when he is not under.. "not the way I want to give them, that is "(Smiles).

So she told Osiris that he now had to undergo a test for his Goddess, a test where what he thinks he feels is a lot less than what is really happening, but it's a pain for his Goddess, and pain for his Goddess he will always undergo with a feeling of lightness .

I wanted to test this.

So I took one of Mistress Lauretta's canes and gave him his first stroke… He let me, I was surprised by the harshness of the thin flexible black rubber coated cane in my hand so I struck again and again and again, I told him I would give him 7 marks, for his Goddess and pain was nothing on the 5th stroke I hit him sooo hard he jumped a meter further and held his hand on his arse. He muttered: "too much pain, too much pain!!! this is too much …"

I looked at Mistress Lauretta and she checked on him to see if he was awake or still under.

She told my friend to take position behind Osiris and informed us that if he is still under he will be asleep in one second and will fall backwards like a stiff piece of wood.

With a snap of her fingers he was put back to sleep and as mistress Lauretta had said he felt straight backwards into the arms of my friend.

We then laid him back on his back on the floor and mistress Lauretta told me that failure or not achieving something is something we sometimes better not share as it's not good for feeding the unconscious, feelings of failure do not contribute to the process of progress.

She said," Maybe try something else now"

I let Osiris smell my perfume and my hair as I sat next to him on the floor, I told him this scent was mine and the smell of my hair would make his dick hard and he would get more and more horny until he would explode… and I repeated this, with a clear voice and repeated what I wanted him to be; "hard for his Goddess and then eventually come for his Goddess "

We enjoyed seeing him grow and grow and getting harder and harder without any touch as he was not allowed to move his hands, So his mind had taken over the job of his hands in order to make him come … he succeeded in this mission and we led him back to the bench .

We told him we were happy with his performance and Mistress Lauretta told him it was slowly about time we woke him up again, but he would not remember anything that was said or none of the actions in his conscious being, it would all stay stored in the subconscious. She went on reassuring him about his state of being after the hypnosis until she ordered him to wake up.

And so he did … We asked him how he felt and he went from tired to feeling very good to feeling very very good and very clear headed but very cold.

I ordered him to kiss my feet and mistress Lauretta's feet and to thank us and especially mistress Lauretta for this wonderful experience he could not remember anything of…

And then he could get dressed and give me my present. In this bag I found my favorite perfume and an envelope with the contribution for mistress Lauretta's work.

We then said goodbye as he needed to head back home and the weather conditions weren't the best and rush hour had set in already.

I told him that I would be the one writing down this experience for a change as he could not.

This was a very successful afternoon.

We sat with mistress Lauretta for a bit longer and had some Champaign and we then went with her into the city where we invited her for dinner.

This hypnosis session will be repeated again soon.

I suspect that due to the hypnosis session I have since then the uncontrollable urge to be more and more on the BDSM networking site to show my submission and other qualifications related to Goddess Ira to a wider public. It is a good idea of my Goddess to have, as with a regular medical check, a regular hypnosis session to deepen my subconscious ties with her to an even higher level.

A few weeks later, after the holidays, I called Osiris to tell him I wanted to see him as there was something missing in the rebuilding of his ego.

We fixed a time to meet and with a delay of fifteen mins he arrived with a very nice present at my place. It were two very beautiful volumes of catalogs of sculpture and he had written a poem in each of them. I have read the poems before but to see them written down in these beautiful books could only add strength to them. It's a lovely feeling to be so worshipped…

We spoke a bit about our writing and I then ordered him to go upstairs and get undressed. He wanted to shower but I told him to wait until after the cleansing the insides process. When that was done and he was clean (in and outside) before me, I ordered him to go into the gynochair with his legs spread and his arse well displayed before me. I then took a vacuum dildo pump that I connected to my vacuum machine and I brought the dildo part into his arse and placed the sucking part around his anus, I then switched on the machine and the dildo penetrated deeper whilst the skin around the anus was pulled out further, in order to create a "pussy" from his arse. I let the machine work like this for about half an hour and then replaced the device by an electro plug, designed for woman.

I told him to get of the chair and move to the bench, I connected the plug to my electro machine and it started going in and out of his "pussy arse" with very steady and firm movements I was in control of the electricity unit and could increase power and speed to my likings.

Then I left the room to pick up some other attributes to make his transformation more complete. I saw Osiris peek to try and find out what it was I was bringing in but I put it all on the floor before he could have a glance.

Then I took big vacuum breast cups and connected them to my machine and placed them over his pierced nipples and breast and switched on the machine, first slowly, then with more power until I felt satisfied about the volume, a nice full B-cup, the machine kept pumping and releasing and over and over again. Then I took a vaginal electro shield and with bondage fixed to cover his sex and testicles as if they were female parts, he screamed when I let the first wave of electricity loose in that area.

The Elevation to Divinity

I enjoyed the sight and thought it was time to start dressing him up, its only then that I told him in order to complete the ego change, I needed to transform him into a replica of myself.

So I started to dress him up, black latex stockings, black latex dress, shoulder length latex gloves and high heels. The outfit I had selected fitted him perfectly; I only needed to add some make-up to his face, the same colors I use and in proportion to his face, in order not to make him look like a drag queen.

I could see his worried face and explained to him what I wanted to achieve: to get him ready for being a copy of me and to assist me today in my domination work.

Osiris muttered a bit but I shut his mouth by covering his face with a neutral color powder which I then diffused with a brush all over his face and neck, followed by shiny lipstick, eye shadow, eyebrow and lashes make-up and blush on his cheeks. I told him I was using the make-up I was wearing myself and that he should be proud to be transformed into my image. Osiris could not do else than agree, although he said that he could never be as beautiful. Of course not, anyone ever could.

As I said to my friend Mistress Lauretta who was staying at my place for a few days, upon Osiris arrival," I am going to transform him into a woman to resemble me as close as possible in order to have a physical and fysical transformation."

The finishing touch was one of my short boblike black wigs. I was pleased with this result and I rewarded Osiris with a bigger size PA from 3.2 to size 4. He did not know why I did this, but I had another intention as well.

I called Mistress Lauretta to come and take a few pictures of me and my look alike, but I noticed that his cock had grown hard and strong and I said I could not be seen with a look alike pointing at me of course, so I put a vibrating device over the top of his dick and let it work on various speeds until he could not do else but give himself to a very nice orgasm.

That was what I needed for the picture, a soft cock I could pull backwards by fixing a small rope through the PA so he would also be feeling like a woman in that region.

With the breast cups still working we then posed for pictures together. When I later disconnected them from the machine they stayed well in place and Osiris looked like a very convincing female, same height as his Goddess, less elegant as it took some effort to walk in high heels of course. But both I and Mistress Lauretta agreed that he looked good enough to be my female assistant in my next session.

This scared him a lot but he knew that there is no point in refusing what is on his Goddess 'mind so he did his best. I could see him trying to do his job as good as possible and I had also made sure it was a short and easy to assist session, but I am sure it had its affect in the physical, visual absorbing of his ego into mine. I could see he looked proud when the client commented about how good he looked.

When the client had left I told him to go back on the bench and I put him into a tighter chastity. It was a lot harder to place it but it would of course be more intense to be sent home like this.

I then removed all the make-up and clothes and sent him to the shower so he could get dressed and ready to make his way home again. However his own underwear he was not allowed to put on. I gave him a black string from soft satin from now on he had to wear a string. It was a constant reminder of his or her changed identity. I also gave him some hypnotic CD's which contained a feminization program to unleash his femininity even more and to increase his confidence as a woman. He had to feel more feminine from the inside out. Before I let him out I had another check if no traces were left and all was ok, green light to go back home before traffic jams were commencing. As always I was impressed by the creativity and inventiveness of my Goddess Ira. But what did I Osiris feel? I know that a physical vanilla love with my Goddess Ira is not possible. But I love her so much that the only remaining option for me was to identify myself as much as possible with my Goddess. Moreover and of more concern this is also very important for her mission. I have to become her "Egyptian soul". I am proud and very grateful that that day she had decided to make me a copy of her. I wish it would have been permanently! There is no greater honor.

The insertion of the vacuum dildo pump into my arse to create a "pussy" felt very good. This feeling was heightened by my imagination. I fantasized that my Goddess created a duplicate of her vagina. For me the submissive of Goddess Ira it felt like a reward. Nowadays everything she does feels like a reward. Just looking at her when she is busy is already a great bonus. By creating a "pussy" on me around my arshole she emasculated me further and strengthened my feminine side. When she put over my pierced nipples the big vacuum breast cups and created a full B-cup I was not only surprised but also very pleased and very proud that they became so large. They looked firm and resembled till a certain extent the strong though much bigger gorgeous breasts of my Goddess Ira. A natural phenomena similar in beauty with the

Garganta del Diablo form Brazil. Which was till I saw her décolleté for the first time for me the most beautiful natural phenomenon I ever had seen? I felt very close to my beloved Goddess. Although it was a little bit painful when you played with the electricity on the vaginal electro shield which you had fixed over my penis and testicles it still felt like a reward.

I loved it that I was made into your look alike. You did choose of course the right attire. I was also immensely pleased and proud that you used your own make-up and applied it on me like you do on your own handsome face. You succeeded that day in my physical and fysical transformation. I felt feminized and I loved to show my love and devotion to you this way. I am now a true believer in female superiority and I listened regular to the hypnotic feminization CD's to increase my feminized traits.

When Mistress Lauretta made pictures of the two of us I was proud to be dressed up like this and to resemble a little bit you. I still remember that I was losing myself into the beautiful poisonous green eyes of you my beloved Goddess while we embraced each other's waist and in the possession of those beautiful breasts with a full B-cup you had created. If I am honest I miss them because they are a reflection of yours. I like to have permanently some of your features. They are a kind of connection that time and distance transcend which I can touch and see when I am not around you and can show of to others who know you. I like to feel permanently you. I felt so proud to be your possession and about you who created me. It was also an honor to assist you with your client. And I was pleased to receive his compliment. I hope in the future to be able to assist you more often. Although my love was not an obstacle it is thanks to your skills and personality that you were able to alter me so fundamentally in my mind and in my appearance. A physical castration and removal of my penis would have been Extreme but much too simple for my Sophisticated Goddess Ira. By assisting you I also became even more aware and identified even more with some of your feelings and thoughts when you performed your work. The chastity device and the enlarged PA is also a powerful reminder.

When I got home my wife made some remarks over my red eyes. I answered they were red because some dust had been blown into them. But we both know they were red because of the applied make-up. Luckily you had been very careful in the removal of the make-up. She believed me. When I that evening looked into the mirror my breasts were still much larger than normal and bore traces of the large vacuum breast pumps. And even today they are a little larger than before. I am truly the creation of my Goddess, her Pygmalion.

Pygmalion

Fundamentally changed forever
It was done clever
She did it gradually
The result is fabulously
I was once a person
Then I met my chiseling surgeon
First I became her property
She girded the collar properly
I was enslaved
I was saved
I was dominated
My Goddess Ira was consecrated
I was subjugated to her gender
She is my shelter
My manhood destroyed
I am overjoyed
Me a void
This I couldn't avoid
I am proud to be her possession
And that I made thanks to her such progression
Her wish is my command
She is the whip hand
Goddess Ira is everything
I am merely her plaything
Forever indebted and in love
She stands in the Universe high above

Osiris

The Elevation to Divinity

I Goddess Ira think I could safely say that with his subjugation the chapter of the ego could be closed satisfactory. To celebrate this milestone and to give him one of my features I made a body etching around Osiris belly button. This body etching is a copy of the tattoo I wear on my belly around my belly button. Many years ago I had devised this tattoo. To make a copy of my Maya tattoo in the form of a body etching on his body was a great honor I bestowed on Osiris.

Body etching is a brand new, fascinating, unique and exotic form of body art. Body etching is done by using a tattoo machine without ink. The mark is precise, distinct and clear. Body etching is essentially making scars in the outer layers of skin which creates beautiful and ornamental scars which in many cases are raised and light or "white" in color. The etching on the body of Osiris may at unexpected times change color and appearances due to alterations in temperature, altitude, barometric pressure and exposure to the sun or tanning. That very thought alone made me smile. Other creative and naughty ideas came to my mind.

The concentric spirals I evenly etched and started just below and very close to Osiris belly button. The first three spirals did flow fluently into each other. The third etched spiral was interrupted at its end by an upwards curling little spiral on the left of the navel of Osiris. If I compare his belly button with a compass it is situated at the north-east. The fourth etched spiral was interrupted at two points. One of these points ended also in an upwards spiralling curl. This curl was a little bit lower situated. If his belly button had been a compass it is located at the south-west. Attached and below to the bottom of this last etched spiral were eight marquesa. The spiral of my tattoo and the spirals of the body etched copy represent eternity.

I took the penis of Osiris in my hands, which immediately became stiff and soon he ejaculated. I rubbed his semen in the freshly created body etching. Then I cascaded my golden shower on it and rubbed my nectar on it and rubbed it also in the freshly created tattoo.

During this session I also put two rings around his nipple and a pin through this nipple. On the other nipple I did the same. I then connected screws to the rings and turned the screws. The effect was that the nipples were stretched. They became at least ten times as long. It was a remembrance of his increasing female traits.

Before he left I put his penis in a chastity device which required a Prince Albert piercing. The cage included a built in cam lock which made the chastity device for Osiris comfortable and discreet. The hooks I used were for a 5 gauge piercing. By using these hooks I stretched the penis of Osiris further. The key I kept and put safely away.

6 Sadistic Goddess Ira in Japan and Egypt.

Thanks to my Goddess, I became who I am today. She changed my norms, values, appearance and makes now the choices for me. I am not any longer jealous and like to show my special relationship with my Goddess to her family and her friends. I am happy when she is happy. I am also thankful that she takes good care of me and protects me whenever she thinks it is needed. I am very fortunate that I have become one of her soul mates. Goddess Ira is a "giant".

Normally it is by being aware of what you think or do that you choose your destination. But in our case it are her thoughts and her actions that determine my destiny. By making my choices and by sharing her thoughts freely with me my karma coincides more and more with her karma. It are our or more precisely her thoughts and actions which ensure that randomness and coincidence don't exist. She created a kind of "twin Karma" which would make it possible for my soul to immerse in her soul. I am indeed very lucky. She now stands for ever firmly at the helm of my life.

I wanted to express my gratitude to her. At home I bundled all my poems which I had made for my Goddess and handed them over to her. My poems reflect the transformation I had undergone. The last poem which I wrote for her was to commemorate the anniversary of my collaring.

Happy anniversary

One year since my collar rest upon my neck
Your collar is forever your blank check
I spoke then my vows loudly

And wear your sign of ownership proudly
You became my owner
My owner who is also my chastener
You own me fully and permanent
I am your adherent
No-one can own me ever again
It is only you who is allowed to hold the rein
Your collar transcends any vanilla marriage
It is a proud sign of your anchorage
I am happy that there is no option of divorce
For me it is a commitment without remorse
Till my last breath
I carry your collar into death
You are one of a kind
That's how you were designed
Precious memories we have woven together
I mostly in the altogether
Our past reflected in writing
A story so exciting
Another year to create
That is our fate
I am yours into infinity
I feel our affinity
New things to enjoy
When I am your toy
Another year to build
Your essence more in me instilled
A new year starts
New endeavours for my private parts
You are my heavenly oasis
You are my basis
You put me on my way
I think of you every day
You are my light, my Moon, my star and my Sun
From you my Goddess I can't shun
You are the most amazing woman I ever knew
A Goddess that made me new
Being your submissive was our choice
In being your property I rejoice

My personality you demolished
To be your sub is a rare price to be cherished
No more embarrassment in front of your friends
I lost my pretends
I lost my jealousy altogether
Thanks to you my diminisher
I know my disposition
Fulfillment through submission
You are my Goddess and I am your submissive
Thanks to you I am alive
We are opposites of the whole
It is you my Goddess who I extol
You control, possess and defend
I please, trust, honor, obey and transcend
Your caring for me is what I crave
I kneel in front of you because I am your property and your slave
You procreated my heart, soul and mind
Through you I shined
I have pledged my submission to your dominance
I am very happy with your predominance
Together we will complete your mission
You take care of our transition

Osiris

I gave my Goddess as a gift a beautiful white long silk nightgown. I knew that this nightgown would enclose her handsome slender body perfectly. My training was then resumed. Goddess Ira asked me about the question Mistress Lauretta had asked me during the hypnosis session. That question was: "Do you fantasize about your Goddess in a way the Goddess has forbidden you to do so and you added is your love for me a healthy one? " I confirmed that I had fantasized about you quite often but that this was a thing of the past since I was changed thanks to her.

I only want to love, to cherish, to admire and to serve you. If I can do that I am happy. I also know that you really value these immaterial gifts. I love you for who you are and what you stand for. That is in my view the most fundamental basis of my relationship with you. That is why I asked you to be your property and to be your sub. That no other woman looks more beautiful than you is of course an extra bonus. Notwithstanding the foregoing it is also of the utmost importance that your mission will be successful. This result overrules all other things.

Part of spiritual illumination is also to be honest with yourself. I asked myself aloud when I was standing in front of you if I was infected with obsessive love. If that where the case we should stop our relationship immediately. The fulfillment of your quest would indeed be impossible and it would also be very destructive for me and you.

It was true that when I had seen you the first time in the sarcophagus I had felt an instantaneous and overwhelming attraction for you. But through our journey through life I have never and will never demand accountability for your activities and I have also no fear of abandonment by you. What's more I don't need to be in constant contact with you but I do love it of course when I receive regularly your attention. Like you I also regret the shortness of the time we have together. I am very proud of you my Goddess and like it when you have contact and meet other persons. You will also lighten up their lives and I will become because of these contacts a richer person. If I was infected with obsessive love it would have expressed itself also with violent actions. There are no physical and mentally violent actions in our (BDSM) relationship which don't belong there and I have no feelings of mistrust because I know your high values and standards. Ergo I am not infected with obsessive love.

You were satisfied with my answer and the chastity device which I wear daily, as a remembrance of my voluntary "castration" for you my Goddess, was removed by you. I had to step into a short leather trouser which was at three points locked with a padlock. I also had to put on leather boots which had at the bottom a kind of metal stirrups. After that my hands were put into leather straps. Connected with a motor hung on the ceiling an iron spreader bar. My Goddess pressed on the button and the spreader bar lowered till it rested on the floor. Goddess Ira grabbed my hands and tied it to this bar. Then she grabbed my left boot and tied it also to the bar. The same she did with my right boot. It was not easy because I am not like my Goddess a very flexible person. Again she pressed the button. This time the spreader bar went up and I was raised in complete agony from the ground. When I hung unprotected in the air she grabbed a whip and I had to keep count of the strokes. But I forgot to count correctly. And so the whipping started again from the start. This time I counted them out loud. She had told me I would receive forty-four beatings. As always Goddess Ira kept her word.

After this treatment she opened the zipper on the back of the leather pants which was due to my position now on the front and pressed the button of the spreader bar. The bar came slightly down until it reached the height of the hips of my Goddess. My Goddess left the room and came back with a long strap-on dildo which she put on. Her eyes were radiant, innocent and she had that lovely smile on her face. She stepped forward and without further introduction she struck the strap in dildo in my ass which was now on the front side the place where women have their pussies. While I was hanging in this uncomfortable position I moved in unison with the moves of my Goddess. I enjoyed looking in her green eyes. It was a delightful feeling to be taken like that by my Goddess. Sometimes of course it did hurt because the strap in dildo was straight and my ass / pussy was curved due to my position in the air. But it was delicious to be taken like this by my Goddess. I was by all means her possession and it felt so close. She was as always in complete control and I was as always completely submissive to her. I yearn for this Absolute Total Power Exchange (APE/TPE) my Goddess has over me. She should disbelieve my words or attitudes if they express something different. The side letter belonging to the property agreement, which eliminated all restrictions, was an additional proof of my yearning of her total control over me. I will always completely obey her and love her above everybody else. I know Goddess Ira is aware of this. It was a pity that after a long time she stopped fucking me.

Again Goddess Ira pressed the button and the bar went down till I was lying on the floor. She disconnected my boots from the spreader bar and I had to spread my legs as far as possible and the irons of the boots were than anchored to the floor. Then she grabbed a rope and tied it onto the Prince Albert piercing and the bar. She did the same with my nipple piercings. Other ropes she attached to the piercings and to the places where my feet were anchored to the ground. Then she pressed the button again. My feet lifted a bit from the ground like the feet of a graceful ballerina. The effect was that the ropes attached to the piercings were stretched taut. Movement was impossible. Goddess Ira began to caress me and pinched my nipples and balls. Finally, she touched with her soft and exquisite hands my penis and started to stroke it. I was ordered not to ejaculated otherwise punishment would follow. She explained that she trained my orgasms. By this training she would ingrain in my psyche that I could in the future only have an orgasm and or ejaculate on her command. Orgasm control or delayed orgasm is not simple. It is quite different form orgasm denial. My focus had to be shifted from having an orgasm to not having an orgasm. Suggestions of Goddess Ira and her knowledge of hypnosis played an important role in this training. The first step towards orgasm on command had been the ceding of my ownership over my orgasms to my Goddess. I had done that in the ownership agreement. I was forbidden to have an orgasm without the express consent and permission of my Goddess. While I was in this "orgasm on command training" she denied me any orgasm. Part of my "orgasm on command training" was to bring me to the brink of an orgasm without the permission to actually have one. Over and over again she was building up the tension in my body and she stretched the limits of my mind control over my body. She would also use the small remote control device belonging to the male management training system and de UBS interface to control me remotely to check and to speed up this process of "orgasm on command training" and other behavioral adjustments. That's what I learned while I was standing on my toes. She introduced a trigger word that had no meaning outside our relationship and explained the purpose of this trigger word. After more "orgasm on command trainings" at her place or at my home, I would have I would have spontaneously an orgasm when she used that word or gave me a command via de UBS interface. Since it was than my first "orgasm on command training" she helped me at the end to achieve an orgasm and to ejaculate. With her hand she fed me my sperm. After that we drank some wine and I was sorry to leave Goddess Ira but also thankful for the way she had taken care of me her property and the Absolute Power she has over me.

This "orgasm on command training" we did regularly and it reinforced the complete control of my Goddess over my orgasms. Time and time again we focused on not having an orgasm than rather on having one. Each time she went a little bit further. After such a tense session she used the trigger word or the UBS interface and I was allowed to have an orgasm. After a few more "orgasm on command training" multiple orgasms followed. Finally my Goddess could whenever she wanted just by using her trigger word even on the phone induce an orgasm in me. I have now, except on the occasion written below, only orgasm on her command.

I am every time I see Osiris surprised by his desire to perform according to my expectations.

As he gets to know me better and therefore also the people close to me, he realizes that if he wants to fit in, it's he who has to and its he who has to want to.

I sometimes regret the shortness of the time we have together as I like the way he has completely submitted to me and the admiration in his eyes.

It would make every woman feel good to be so admired, respected and adored.

But it all seems to have gone so very smoothly, all with a smile, looking back on the past months.

Our conversations about ancient cultures, rites and all the processes we have gone through and we still have to face are opening my receptors again for information that had been stored away for a while. And in a way without realizing I have been going deeper into inner-searching myself again. Going back to the centerpoint and let that also influence my decisions and the way I spend my time.

From my own centerpoint I can achieve more by using less energy to get there and I've recently started feeling a new and stronger balance inside myself.

Balance is something each individual has to aim for and should not be confused with calming down… I will always be active in mind and body, so calming down is not what I have been doing. I am just wasting less energy in outburst or explosions (not in aggression that can be just as well as in passion) but I divide my energy and use it with more elegance.

It's like I have come to appreciate myself in another way, a more mature way I dare say.

It's like I write down my thoughts before I read them out loud.

I enjoy solitude more than I used to and nature and sports. But the more refined ones like ballet, yoga, Pilates where I have to be in control over the energy I give my body to become as light as a feather. That's how my head feels as well, like the daily stress can only enter partly and will not affect the lightness of being.….

I am looking forward to travel to explore further how light I can get and how open I can be to be even more enlightened.

What people call "my darkness" has always been light for me as I enjoyed and enjoy it with a smile and with great pleasure.

It is good to feel so good.

It is good to be surrounded by just a few "real" people, instead of wasting my time teaching others how to see the light in "my darkness", unaware that they are trying to blind me.…

Osiris has helped creating this awareness by his devotion and his complete submission on a very high spiritual level.

A few days later Goddess Ira called me and used the secret code which she had tattooed on my pubic. I was immediately in trance. When I went after your phone call to bed I didn't remove my PA chastity device which

Goddess Ira and Osiris

I normally do. It is a safety precaution I always take because my wife is sleeping beside me. I fell immediately into a deep trance. I saw that I had no clothes on and that I stepped into a large round golden cage. This cage with me in it went up high into the sky. The landscape changed continually. I flew above large parts of Western Europe. I flew over the ancient Italian cities of Rome, Pompeii and Syracuse and across the Mediterranean See. I flew over the Egyptian city Alexandria and saw the pyramids. Finally the golden cage started to descend at a temple complex in the south of Egypt.

When the cage had landed the door of the cage opened and I stepped out. There I met a slender naked woman with black hair and green eyes. She walked towards me and entered into my body. My body changed into her body and I knew instantly that this was the Goddess Isis. I know that Isis represents the unconscious will, the hidden desires. She or we walked towards a large stair consisting of twenty descending steps. We went down the stairs envisioning and concentrating on the "red triangle with snake" tattoo which Goddess Ira had put on the first chakra till this chakra became very hot. After that we concentrated on the next chakras and it's by Goddess Ira tattooed symbols while descending the stairs. Halfway down the light faded away completely and we were plunged in total darkness. Finally when all chakras were feeling hot we entered a large circular room. This room was filled with statues. In the middle there was a large bed which we occupied. This bed was at the middle bent and had at its feet an elevated side. This was a bed used by the nobility in ancient Egypt. Because it was bent in the middle you couldn't fall out of it. The pillow was of stone and was decorated with images and the names of Isis and Osiris. Around the bed were four man-sized candles burning. We saw that the statues came to life. It seemed like that they were moving and I am convinced that they were standing besides the bed. All of the statues had the head of an Egyptian deity. They started to chant in a language I didn't recognize. It was hypnotizing.

The energy level in our body was now very high. Our body felt terribly hot and without any substance. The energy went down through the left side of our body and ascended via the chakras through our spinal cord. We felt clearly the rising of the kundalini. The coiled snake was moving. Finally it reached our brain's central nervous system and endocrine command center. Our whole body was one erogenous zone. It seemed as if our body floated and had become limitless. Our whole body was in ecstasy. No we were ecstasy. We had a very intense orgiastic experience. It was a multi orgiastic event which can only be described as a mind shattering bliss. We had full body orgasms. Although there was of course no ejaculation our body secretion did for some time, like a slowly rippling river, flow out of our body. After that I woke up and my wife hadn't noticed a thing and I felt a very large pool of body fluid on my pubic. This body fluid smelled and tasted like my sperm which I found strange while the PA chastity device doesn't allow an erect penis and I thought to remember that we had a whole range of body orgasms. An ejaculation with the PA chastity device on is even impossible.

Later I learned from Goddess Ira that she had given me when she used the secret code some instructions. However she hadn't used the trigger word. I am very grateful that I had this experience and that Goddess Ira takes so good care of my sensual physical and mental needs. The earlier teachings of Dewi were of course also very helpful in understanding what had happened.

It was strange that this trance happened to Osiris just at the time that I myself had started meditating because I had to free myself of having absorbed too much negative energy, I could feel the negative energy in my calf's and I had to go back to the centerpoint, through a ritual of my body chakras and through breathing to let this heavy feeling escape my body and let it go completely empty in able to be filled with fresh clean air .

At that moment we were oceans apart in a completely different timezone and I did not use any of my control devices to involve Osiris in this cleansing ritual, but he felt it nevertheless and how!

It's not only the tolerance of pain and the seeing him struggle through the humiliation that gives me pleasure; it's also that invisible bond that is branded into his body as a platform to exchange our energy fields.

A few weeks later Honey and I received instructions from the Goddess to report to Kioshi in Japan. We landed at the airport of Tokyo and we felt that were expected. We grabbed a taxi which brought us to a large shopping mall in downtown Tokyo.

Shortly after we arrived a man and a woman entered the mall. I thought that I recognized them from the airport. We took the elevator to the top floor and also the man and this woman took the elevator and they left also at the top floor. I was not yet completely convinced that we were followed. But I didn't want to take unnecessary risks. We went directly via the stairs one floor down, they did likewise. It was now clear that we were followed. They had to belong to one of the secret societies the Maya legend warned about.

I whispered in the ear of Honey that we were followed and that she should step into the elevator and press the button for the ground floor. In the meantime I blocked the entrance of the elevator. When the door was almost closed I jumped into the elevator. They ran also to the elevator but were too late. At the ground floor we almost ran to the entrance of the shopping mall. When we arrived in the mall I had noticed the entrance of a subway. At random we took a train. At the next stop we got out and took a taxi. After a few miles we changed taxis. The last one took us to the outskirts of Tokyo. There we rented under a phony name a car and went to the place at the appointed time to report to mister Kioshi.

It was full moon. Our companion took us to Mount Fuji. This mountain is the highest mountain in Japan, rising to 12388 feet and visible from Tokyo and is one of the most holy places for the Japanese people. It is a volcano created 600000 years ago. It is a gateway to another world a gateway to the Gods. He brought us to an abandoned mine. We went inside. Our companion left us there at the entrance. He hadn't said much. It was spooky and silent. We were waiting quite a long time before we met Akina. She introduced herself as the geisha Akina. She told us that her name means fountain, flower. Suddenly I heard your voice. I was surprised and looked around me but I could not find you. You said to me that it was OK to follow her. I doubted myself. But then I felt a strong power surge through my collar. I couldn't remove my collar since you my Goddess had the key with which the collar was locked. That power surge was the deciding factor to follow Akina.

A geisha is not a prostitute. A geisha is a special companion. It involves a long training to become a geisha. The training takes place in an Okiya or geisha house. It is a thorough and serious training in conversation, in music, dance and in playing musical instruments. She told me that Katsu was her danna. A danna is a person who visits her often and supports her financially. Akina gives Katsu sexual favors in turn. However today it is her role to entertain us. It is her duty to put me and Honey at ease.

Akina grabbed a torch and brought us further into the mine. Soon I lost all sense of direction. Everywhere were abandoned shafts. Sometimes we went up sometimes we went down. Sometimes she used antiquated lifts. The air in the mine was stale and damp.

Eventually we arrived in a large cavern. The cave was sparsely light with torches. Nevertheless I could see that there was a beautiful large green lake and a large statue of an ancient Goddess. In front of her there was a white marble altar. On the altar there were two blue candles and white flowers. In a semi circle around the alter were tea lights placed.

In the cave Honey and I met Katsu the danna of Akina. Akina explained that he is, in the ancient way, a specialist tattooist and the high priest of the Goddess Fuji a fire Goddess. When she spoke about the fire Goddess she pointed her middle finger in the direction of the large statue. Katsu wore a golden robe which reached to his ankles. On the back was embroidered in red a bright flame.

Katsu explained that a ritual cleansing in the presence of the Goddess had to take place. Katsu gave Honey and me the assignment to undress which we did. Honey looked very appealing with her small breasts, shapely buttocks and spindly legs. You could see that her mother once had been a beauty queen. Honey had inherited her genes. Her three tattoos were barely visible. Her piercings were removed. Also my tattoos and brands were hardly recognizable. I was allowed to keep on my collar and the piercings in my dick and in the nipples but the PA chastity device had to be removed. With the key Honey had received from Goddess Ira she unlocked my chastity device. In the meantime Akina was preparing the tea. Katsu invited us to join him. Honey and I accepted the offered tea and drank the cup quietly empty. The tea was delicious but had an odd flavor. Later I learned it was to diminish the pain and to enhance our spirits.

Katsu instructed Honey and me to step into a circle in front of the altar and to look into the flame of a candle. Then he began to sing in a language unknown to us. At the outside of the circle Akina was dancing an ancient rhythmical dance. If I have to guess it took at least several hours. During that whole time we were not allowed to move and had to stare into the flames.

Suddenly he stopped with the incantations and Akina with her dance. Again we were invited to drink the odd tea. After this we were ordered to walk into the green lake and to stay under water for approximately one minute. Again I heard your voice. Was I losing my mind? Your voice said do as you are told. The water was so cold that we had immediately goose pimples on our skin. The ancient Japanese ritual could continue.

The name Katsu means firm, hard. While Katsu prepared his tools he explained to me the difference between the electrical method of making tattoos and the ancient Japanese tattoo method. The ancient Japanese tattoo method is called tebori. Literally it means tattooing by hand. One of the hardest parts about learning tebori is not just the skill of making the tools but also how to use them. Because Katsu is a traditional Japanese master in tebori he holds the handle of his tools at the far end. This is quite difficult.

Special tattoos are administered only by priests or holy monks. It is an

Goddess Ira and Osiris

esoteric art which provides the wearer indelible protection from a variety of misfortunes. It is also has mystical power to influence other people's behavior. These special tattoos are a prerequisite for marriage and for the afterlife. The power of the inscription ultimately depends upon the level of power embodied in the tattooist who gives it. Tattoos have power because they not only draw on the power of the tattooist, but also of his predecessors. You can't take getting or giving this kind of tattoo lightly. The priest has to be mentally and physically prepared every time he does it.

When he prepared his tablet I saw that he used a set of razor sharp bamboo sticks. It was clear to me that he would put a Japanese tattoo on me. But I had no clue were. These bamboo sticks would puncture my skin that was clear. I was instructed to lie down on the altar. He fixed ropes around me. Again I felt a strong power surge through my collar. Akina started again to make music and to dance around the altar. It was wonderfully relaxing although I was afraid of the strong power surge which went sometimes through my collar. However this tranquil mood abruptly changed when Katsu told me that he would tattoo the name of my Goddess on my dick. And in your genital area I will also tattoo seven words he said.

I, as the Goddess of Osiris, had given the photo from the earlier session to Katsu as how to sculpt the genitals of Osiris. I had asked him to do it the tebori way. He put a ball splitter on and I saw that he tightened the ball splitter significantly. The penis of Osiris was by now pretty long since it was stretched again by an iron chain with the nipples and the ring of the collar. It was indeed an ideal place for my signature. As his Goddess I had chosen the color brown. It was obviously a great honor to leave your name at that particular place. Osiris didn't know that I had hidden myself in the cave.

Osiris was distracted from Katsu because Akina started to undress. She did wear a distinctive red underkimono. It fitted her like a second skin and was tied down with a golden cord around her waist. I also noticed her special white socks and her zori sandals. These socks separates the big toe form the other toes.

Her face was white with a thick white make-up. This white substance covered almost all visible part of her skin, including her chest and neck. The nape of the neck had the typical W or V shape of clear skin which had no white make-up. Her lips were red. Her eyebrows and eyes were drawn with traditional charcoal. The eyebrows and the corners of her eyes were colored black. She also had a little bit of red around her eyes. Her long black hair was down to her waist and oiled.

Akina told me when my danna is working on your penis it will hurt a

The Elevation to Divinity

lot. It is important to relax and to have fun with me. This will diminish your pain. Then she gave me a kiss on my mouth. Although it were not the lips of my Goddess it tasted great. She had used the traditional red color which had crystallized sugar in it. She told me how the lipstick was made. Now I understood why the geisha's kisses are so sweet.

Again she pressed her lips against my lips and started with her tongue to explore my mouth. She asked Honey to join us and so the three of us were losing ourselves in kisses. I imagined that I was kissing my Goddess. This was not so difficult since I heard at regular intervals her sweet voice. At a certain moment Honey made from her mouth a sucker and sucked hard on my genital area. It left red dots. It was very pleasant. Nevertheless my thoughts were mainly with my Goddess. My love and soul belonged to her and I had because of that deep and unbreakable bond second thoughts. Was it okay that I enjoyed myself? My Goddess knew me better than I did while I did hear at that moment her sweet voice saying enjoy yourself Osiris I am with you. I am you. While we were kissing we brought hot and cold candy in the mouth of our kissing partners. I even got fellatios with icy tongues from both of them.

After a while Akina rested her bottom on my mouth. Nevertheless I saw and noticed the tattooist dip his needle in the ink. To increase my feeling awareness Honey put a blindfold before my eyes. Then I felt the pressing of the needles rapidly and rhythmically into my cock. As the cutting intensified I felt that the blood was wiped away. At a certain moment he paused and when he started again the rhythm had changed. It felt different. I could smell the scent of my Goddess and heard her voice before me. The tattooist was singing an epic poem and reciting a kind of spell or magic formula. These invocations were symbolically significant. Fuchi, the fire goddess was invoked because communication with other deities and spirits was impossible without her intervention. Fuchi lent her spiritual support in times of trouble and at times of death. The voices in my head were still whispering. I just wanted to please and to serve my Goddess. I only wanted to be with my Goddess. I wanted to see, hear and feel my Goddess because I was already over a long period emotionally completely addicted to my Goddess. Nobody can stand in her shadow but Akina and Honey were good substitutes. When I was brooding on these thoughts I heard suddenly the voice of my Goddess in my ear. "What you do for them you do for me. It is okay to have fun with Akina and Honey." In spite of her sweet voice with that irresistible southern accent I still had second thoughts. I loved my Goddess and I was the property of my Goddess but I found it strange that her fragrance was so clearly there. Again I heard her voice: "You obey me completely. The higher your pleasure the higher the surrender to me. Do not run from the night when you ask for the moon. Do not walk away from the thorns if you ask for a rose" I understood her message. The thorns of the rose symbolized of course that love is not always easy and that it needs effort to make my love for my beloved Goddess everlasting. The rose itself of course stands for her unprecedented beauty and her continuous love but the rose also stands for death and rebirth. The moon stands for the protection I receive from my Goddess when I escort her on her journey through life.

Although only a few characters were made it took more than an hour and hurts a lot more than the electrical needles. The pain was different. I had a strong feeling that my Goddess was with me. Was I losing my mind? I didn't know if it was because my thoughts were with my Goddess but my pain disappeared like snow before the sun. I remembered her words. What you do for them you do for me. In my mind Akina and Honey swapped positions with my Goddess. That gave me the peace of mind to follow and accept the direct order of my Goddess which she had transmitted.

With my blindfold still on I started licking and gently sucking around the mouth of Akina's vaginal entrance. I started slowly. I used my tongue to lick her vagina from its entrance up to her clitoris. I moved my tongue from the inner lips to her outer labia on one side. Then I started to draw her lips into my mouth and to massage them with my tongue. After that I moved to the other side. In the meantime I noticed that Honey was kissing Akina. I imagined her kissing the neck of Akina. I know that this is for most women a very erotic place. I also imagined that they were kissing each other's nose, ears and eyes. Sometimes they changed place while I repeated my activities with the other woman. I felt a little soft silk cloth rubbing my nose. I remembered that the silk cloth smelled like my Goddess and I found the odor in the silk cloth overpowering. This intensified my thinking of my Goddess. All the time my body was fixed tightly on the white marble altar. I felt that the ropes around my arms were freed a bit.

After that I moved my tongue in and out of Akina's slit. Sometimes I took a break to explore her insides again. But if I stopped to long I felt the power surge through the collar and I heard the order of my Goddess to continue. I varied in conjunction with the tattooist my cadence and the firmness of my tongue. A firm tongue I used to circle her clitoris. When I covered more ground I used a limber more flat tongue. But again and again I returned to her clitoris. Each time I started out gently and increased the pressure and the speed in accordance with her body language, the cadence of the tattooist, the power surge through the collar and the voice of my Goddess. Akina became really hot. On the now swollen clitoris I gave quick little sucks by putting the clitoris in my mouth and releasing it time and time again. By now her whole body was shaking. However Honey did also not forget me. She grabbed a piece of my skin between her teeth and pulled it very gently. Then she let it go and started again with a new piece of my skin. She did not start immediately to bit hard but gradually she built it up. Eventually the biting was so venomous that I had to scream.

In the mean time I also used my tongue and my fingers to go over and around the clitoris of Akina. My arms where still bound but could move a little. This latitude was enough to use my fingers. I made sure that I was not thrusting my fingers too deep or too fast. At a certain moment I used my finger to rub her G-spot. This G-spot felt a little bit rough and was located on the anterior wall of the vagina. Whit my blindfold still on it was easier to feel and stimulate her. Then all of a sudden she ejaculates all over my mouth. The name Akina (fountain) is very well chosen! This stimulated Honey and she couldn't refrain herself any longer. She powerfully grabs my head by my hair and starts passionately to kiss me on my mouth. She got ecstatic when she tasted the silver nectar of Akina.

Almost at the same time the tattooist is ready with my dick. My blindfold was removed and there I saw you with a tattoo tool in your hand. I can't describe how happy I was to see you. I knew immediately that it was you who had been the tattooist. You later confirmed this to me. At the basis of my penis, in a half circle you had tattooed a Japanese name. As an experienced jeweler that name was now for ever delicately engraved onto my dick.

The priest of ancient cultures believed that knowing the real name of somebody or of an object gave spiritual power over it. Once the priest knew the name it was within his power to destroy or to let the person or the object to live for eternity. This power which is locked in the ancient wisdom that relates to the "knowledge of names" is doubled when the name is written down. That day you acquired that double power over my penis. My penis has now a name and only you know what that name is. Your ownership stamp is on it.

You said aloud "that from now on it is for all to see that your cock not only belongs to me your Goddess but is also part of me." An immense gratitude came over me that you had chosen my dick, my most intimate part, to permanently inscribe with a name full of special significance. What an incredible honor to cede my penis to you. From that moment on it was "you" who fucked. If I had to pee it was "you" who peed. Metaphysically you had become a hermaphroditic who can pollinate herself. Also my most intimate part as a man was from that moment on taken from me and became part of my Goddess. Also this was a major step in reframing my soul.

Then Katsu took over the tattoo tool which you had in your hand and started to tattoo seven words on my crotch with invisible UWV white ink from the bottom to the top. There was no pain I felt happy. You were with me. Honey started rubbing my tattooed penis and balls while Akina was kissing me. Honeys squeezed my balls just a little. She and Honey were kissing me alternately. Eventually Honey put herself on her knees between my legs. She took again my penis in her hand. She stroked it gently and used her thumb to tease the head of my cock. Then finally she leaned forward to lick just the tip. With her hands on my thighs and her thumbs rubbing my balls she began to tease me. Alternating she licked my balls and the head of my cock. She did this very gently. My tattooed cock responded, grew and hardened more and more with each lick of Honey. And I was happy you were with me and all the time I smiled to you. You told me later that my face was radiant and glowing. This doesn't surprise me beloved Goddess I saw you in front of me and you are my light that I cherish and love.

Finally Honey wrapped her lips around me. She paused a moment to taste my pre-cum. She swirled her tongue around as she put the slightest amount of pressure on her lips. Then she began to suck. I responded rather quickly. I wanted to please you as a spectator at this event. You were smiling and with that you encouraged me to let lose all constraints. Sometimes I moaned or gasped. She sucked only the end of my penis. I wanted more. I wanted all of her mouth. Her hands were still working. Rubbing my balls and squeezing them. Finally Honey plunged her head down all the way. I wanted to come. But I couldn't. She tugged on my sack to make sure that it didn't happen. I had my hands on her head and ran my fingers through her hair. But my eyes locked with your eyes and I did drown in them. Meanwhile Honey moved up and down on my shaft with different speed. I got very close to an orgasm. She pulled back. Katsu was working on the last word. Time was getting close. She moved one hand under my sack and began to apply pressure to that place just above my ass. She sucked harder and harder, faster and faster. Her tongue was swirling. At that same time you used the internal processor low on my spinal highway near my tailbone. My rectal muscles squeezed rhythmically. Akina was passionately kissing my mouth and face which was still partly covered with her juices. You said the trigger word and then I came with full force and I sprayed down her throat, filling her mouth with my hot juices. Honey loved it. She wanted it all and she kept her lips around my dick until I had given all I had. She swallowed all of it down. You then said I promised "that If you obey me completely your pleasure will increase and the higher your pleasure the higher your surrender to me. But never forget that loving me is your only possibility and that your soul, mind and body are mine. You belong only to me."

I can focus again and see from the bottom to the top that Katsu had tattooed the words Generous, Obedience, Devoted, Dedicated, Emotional, Submissive and Spiritual in my genital area. These words were integrated with the branding you had made in the session before the collaring. Those words were more or less antonyms of your seven qualities: Gorgeous, Original, Dangerous, Dominant, Extreme, Sadistic, Sophisticated.

The next morning Honey and I were expected to leave at 4 o clock. Before we left we all had a meditation session with Akina and Katsu. During this meditation Honey felt a little sick. Since Katsu was a high priest he was also skilled in naturopathy. Honey asked Katsu what was wrong with her. After a brief investigation Katsu concluded that she was pregnant. We all understood immediately that this could only mean that she was conceiving my baby. This could complicate my life further. I thought back to the moment of conception at your place when we were with Dewi. The moment when life and death come together and forge a chain that connects thousands of generations before us which thousands of generations to come. My intercourse with Honey was thus connected with the sensual, with death and with my Goddess Ira. Goddess Ira had devised it. She had created life and plays therefore a very prominent and distinct role in that chain of thousands of generations. Only when that chain ends Goddess Ira's role is played in this respect. If you consider this occurrence from that perspective it is breathtaking. Only Goddess Ira could with her creativity and high intelligence make such a responsible choice. To develop such a plan requires not only courage but also a personality that transcends the bourgeois milieu in which we ordinarily live. A choice like that can only be based on the most exceptional values.

In my mission to save the world I will have to create something that grows, a seed that will flower and become another source of life, a generation younger than my own daughter.

And who better to choose for that mission than my two very loyal devote ones.

I had assured Honey that we would all take up our responsibilities in the education and bringing up of our perceived fruit and that she will never have to worry or make decisions on her own as we will all be there for her, mentally, sometimes physically, financially and emotionally.

The idea to create a baby who is brought up by several parents came to me a few years ago, looking at the youth of today, more than half of them has lived in altered nucleus, in a way they get four parents, eight grandparents, more brothers and sisters, but they don't choose for this themselves.

If we would have the possibility to make that choice up front and divide our responsibilities towards the child, bring it up in all different parts of the world in different stages of life, to be surrounded by another warmth and comfort being a baby under the warm sun, to be educated by a man partly in another continent, to be presented to different lifestyles and to learn about darkness and light and to acquire skills no others have by a Goddess who seems to travel through time in a way….A multicultural child, multi habitual, multilingual, multiintelligent…A creation of us and a responsibility.

Honey felt honored I had chosen her, never has she doubted my natural ability to command without words, always she has listened to her inner voice that assured her I would bring her happiness and adventure and completeness whilst her brain tried to warn her for the dangers that I would introduce her too… Well they are certainly least of Honeys worries now, she looks ever so happy…. I feel like a creator now, I have created happiness in her, happiness in Osiris, although I know he worries about how this will affect his life as he knows it ..I will assure him that he does not have to worry, our mission is of a much higher significance and he will learn about that much sooner than he is aware of now.

Finally it was time to leave. Akina lit a torch and we left the cave. The temperature there, deep down in the earth hadn't changed. Soon I lost all orientation. We went left and right and vice versa. Up and down. We took several times again the antique elevators. After a long journey we reached the entrance of the mine. It was still dark. We were met there by Kioshi. He was wearing a large backpack with ropes. Katsu had given us the instruction to enter the volcano. If we followed his instructions we would find the designated place and the box of stone.

It was a long climb to the summit. The mountain was covered in snow. The temperature was deep below zero. By the end of the day Kioshi stopped. From his backpack he took his mountain equipment which he gave to me. He also gave me protective clothing. I had to go down alone tonight. Kioshi warned me. The inside of the volcano is treacherous. It's not uncommon that volcanologist take a wrong step and sink below the surface. This happened last week. Within seconds he was burned till his waist. He was lucky that his colleague managed to save him otherwise he would have sunken deeper and burned completely. That is why the Goddess Fuji received in ancient times the name fire goddess.

After several hours of resting it was time to leave. I said goodbye to Kioshi and kissed Honey. Would I see you, her and the baby again? I went down in the volcano. If all went well I would be back again tomorrow morning. I took my flashlight and followed the instructions of Katsu. During the descent I used frequently my cane. It was a needed precaution. Quite often the cane disappeared and burnt a little. The more I descended the warmer the temperature became. After some time I put on the protective clothing. That was necessary since the temperature had risen to approximately 100 degrees Celsius. Now and then I stopped to catch my breath and to drink some hot water. But there was not much time. I knew that I had to be out of the volcano before daylight. If not I would certainly die. Finally I arrived at the designated spot.

I took the spade from the backpack and began to dig. After I had dug a deep pit I hit something hard. Then I used my hands to dig further. Despite the protective gloves my hands were blistering from the heat. But I kept on going. I found a box made from stone. I tried to open the box but this was not possible. I put the box into my backpack and started the difficult journey back. I looked up into the sky and saw that I would not be able to reach the edge of the volcano in time. Not even if I ran. Nevertheless I started to run as fast as I could and hoped that I would imagine an escape and would not fall into one of those treacherous pits. It was almost dawn. A mile or two in front of me I saw an overhanging cliff. And then in a flash you my Goddess did appear. You told me to use my phone and to ask Kioshi to lower a rope from the edge of the cliff. So I did. I phoned Honey and she gave the phone to Kioskhi. Hurriedly I told him how he could save me. There was not much time left and I didn't know for sure if Kioskhi had understood me. When I came to the cliff there was no rope. I screamed. It had become very, very hot. The protective clothing was almost burning and all over my skin I felt blisters. Suddenly with a deep thud the rope fell a few meters from me. I tied the rope around my waist and gently pulled the rope. Kioshi started to pull. But he could not pull me up. He enlisted the help of Honey. And together they were able, however with great difficulty, to pull me up.

I was exhausted but we had to go on quickly. At the entrance of the mine the box was handed over to Akina who was waiting. Katsu would send the stone box by special courier to Charlotte.

We were brought into the mine again. Akina was our guide once more and after some time we arrived at a complex of caves.

There were you again, my Goddess. You were accompanied by Eeshain. Her name was derived from the goddess Parvati and means purity. The Hindu goddess Parvati symbolizes with the Hindu god Shiva the power to create and to destroy. Eeshain was a voluptuous woman with long black hair, a dark skin and green eyes.

She told us what the rules were during our stay: no sex, meat, alcohol, drugs or cigarettes. I had to undress in front of her and she put a cream on my blisters. Our stay in the cave complex was dictated by regular activities. The activities were a mix of meditation, yoga, satsang, chanting and meals. The meals were vegetarian and always purified. There was also personal time for whatever we choose to pursue. My skin healed extremely fast. Eeshain gave me every week two paired words to meditate. I knew them already very well but during my personal time I had to contemplate these pared words further. We stayed in the cave complex for seven weeks. The words she had given me were: Gorgeous and Generous, Original and Obedience, Dangerous and Devoted, Dominant and Dedicated, Extreme and Emotional, Sadistic and Submissiveness, Sophisticated and Spiritual. By contemplating on these words I was able to notice more and more the essence behind these words and their mutual interdependence.

A highlight of the day or was it night was the satsang. Satsang means "search of truth". These gatherings toke about two hours. After that Eeshain sat in one of the caves with a waterfall behind her to answer questions from us. This is the ancient method used for spiritual instruction. During our stay I saw Honey only at these satsangs and the subsequent meetings.

Eeshain explained during these meetings to us that it is our daily lifestyle that gives rise to negative emotional states. Ignorance and Ego form the real basis of all pains and suffering. It is our modern lifestyle that leads to more and more independence. Due to this lifestyle we move toward exclusiveness. This increases the duality and makes our Ego stronger. The life in this cave complex is directed to an expansion of your awareness to overcome your Ego or what is left of it. I therefore encourage perfecting your thoughts, words and deeds.

I learned that every experience should prod me to witness it with awareness. I should constantly witness my feelings and try to go deeper by understanding why I feel particularly so. When you do this you will realize that the fault is not in the environment or in the people that you interact with. Instead the problems arise mostly from within. At regular intervals I felt the power surge through my collar and sometimes I could feel the ground shake. I then knew that an earthquake had occurred. I remember clearly that one was extremely powerful and that I was afraid.

During the seven week I had once a week a special meeting with Eeshain and my beloved Goddess in her personal quarters. This was the only time during the week I saw my Goddess. I craved for this moment. Emotionally and physically I am completely submissive to her. But I was also lucky since I quite often heard your voice in my head when I was meditating. You had ample time to profoundly influence and indoctrinate me with your thoughts and feelings in this seclusion. We needed this time to mold my Ba, Ka and Sheut further. Eeshain always wore a white top which was tightly fixed around her voluptuous torso. The white top had a large slit on the front. She had tattooed a large red cross on her body. The vertical tattoo started at her throat and ended at her clitoris. The horizontal tattoo was from one side of her waist to the other side of her waist. Her dark legs were bare. The first time I saw her dressed like that I asked her why she had tattooed a large red cross on her body. She told me then that the cross represented the union of divinity (the vertical line) and the world (the horizontal line). Parvati has like me also a more fierce appearance and she is then known as the goddess Kali. She is the only goddess to which blood is scarified. That is why the cross on my body is red. Eeshain is a Hindu priestess and a qualified Ayurvedic physician. Her room was always dimply lit. I always had to disrobe and to lay on a table where I covered my groin area with a towel.

Ayurvedic medicine is a Hindu medical system. In Ayurveda there are three basic substances. These are wind, bile and phlegm. Occasionally blood was added as the fourth. According to Ayurvedic medicine there is equilibrium when one is born. But most people lose it quickly. They lose it either by bad diet, bad treatment or by moving away from the physical location most conductive to their natural constitution and temperament.

All diseases and disabilities results from an excess or deficit of one of these basic substances. When one is suffering from a surplus or imbalance of one of the basic substances his or her personality and physical health is affected. The purpose of an Ayurvedic physician is to discover what the optimum conditions might be and to try to keep that optimum.

The primary method for returning and maintaining the basic elements in the optimum state is diet. The Goddess has brought me to this cave complex to be cleaned and to be purified mentally and bodily by Eeshain. I had to drink a brew of dietary fibers, herbs, supplements and dietary laxatives. The brew also consisted of a fluorescent liquid a kind of liquid gold. It tasted a little bit salty and had a flavor that was vaguely familiar. But I couldn't identify it. Every week the liquid became more golden. Her Colon cleansing dietary plan was aimed to support cleansing my colon, removing food, increasing circulation to clear toxic and provide nutrition to my main organs which are involved in the process of detoxification. After that you and Eeshain left the room for some time.

When you both came back, you hooked up an enema and Eeshain asked me to remove the towel and to raise my buttocks into the stirrups. I then felt your hand parting my bottom cheeks and then I felt some lubricant being spread on my anus. This was followed by a slow insertion of the speculum. This colon cleansing was also aimed at removing feces and nonspecific toxins from my colon and intestinal tract.

An enema was used to inject water mixed with herbs and other liquids into my colon and into my rectum via my anus. The increasing volume of the liquid caused rapid expansion of my lower intestinal tract resulting in a very uncomfortable bloating, cramping and powerful peristalsis. There was a feeling of extreme urgency and complete evacuation of the lower intestinal tract.

Sometimes enemas are forcibly applied as a mean of punishment. Sometimes you both did punish me. It was when I had not followed your instructions completely. Then Kali showed in Eeshain and my blood was offered to Kali and I had to drink some of your blood. However enemas can be pleasurable and can stimulate the prostate gland. I had unexpected erections which embarrassed me slightly in front of Eeshain. I surrendered to my body's deepest call to release all that I did not longer need. Eeshain combined the treatment with sensual tantra massage while you were watching. She proceeded to massage my colon and my abdomen as the fluid came in me. The Ayurvedic medical wisdom describes a system of erogenous zones or points of arousal. These points are enumerated in texts such as the Kama Sutra and Ananga Range. But these points are also used in the martial arts.

After some time you both left again and came back some time later. I had then to empty my bladder. Eeshain then stirred in my shit. She muttered something to herself. At first we could see no change. But when we stayed longer in the complex of caves the collar of my excrement became lighter and lighter. In week seven there was a triumphant shout of you both. The golden brew which I had been given a few hours earlier had not changed

The Elevation to Divinity

in my body. The liquid had retained its color. Eeshain said solemnly "you are now purified and completely cleaned from all guilt and you have done your penance." And to Goddess Ira she said "the end of your mission lies as you know in Mexico and Osiris is ready."

She yelled to Akina and instructed her to get Honey as soon as possible in her personal quarter. Meanwhile she took the golden excrement in her hands while casting spells and started to make a bracelet out of my golden shit. My shit was transformed into twenty-four carat gold. Honey entered the room. Eeshain put the snake bracelet around the left arm of Honey. Eeshain explained to Honey that the bracelet was a powerful protection amulet. Remember that as long as you life it can't be removed.

From my golden shit she also had made a golden hanger in the form of the sun. The golden hanger you my Goddess hung around my neck and you said: "The living receiver brings back the artifact ". We both knew that this amulet could only be removed by you when the circumstances were right. Eeshain instructed us that if the circumstances were not right I would die and could not be resurrected. Then the quest of my beloved Goddess would be a failure. I felt weird. I felt changed. It felt as if every cell in my body was alien. I had become a pure person. My appearance had changed. Because of this change in appearance my identity papers could be a problem.

From the remaining shit Eeshain made golden coins. These coins could only be used to pay or to bribe during our travel to intermediate stop Egypt and end destination Mexico. You asked Honey if she was still willing to bring me to Egypt. She nodded her accord. You Goddess Ira had urgently to transact some business at home and would travel directly to your home. Only if we found something of interest or when you were needed would you come to Egypt.

Because I had changed so much my identity papers were almost worthless. We all started planning the journey to Egypt. Honey and I went to the airport of Tokyo. When we stood in front of the check-in counter we noticed our old friends form the mall who were looking to Honey. The woman went away while the man was watching us closely from some distance. We received our labels and our luggage had been put on the tape. At that moment a man from the security came to us and asked us to follow him. We were brought to a special room full of electronic devices. We were scanned and searched. We even had to undergo an internal examination. Against this practice I made serious objections. I told them that Honey was pregnant. They just smiled and continued. It looked to me that they enjoyed it. I hoped that this internal examination would not hurt the baby.

Meanwhile our luggage was also checked. After it became clear that we had nothing with us that warranted a longer arrest or delay they had to let us go. But before we could go a Japanese official had written in our passports in capital letters that we were no longer welcome in Japan because of suspicious activities. We were barely in time for our flight to Cairo. And to be honest I was shaking, upset and very angry.

Of course I knew that what the Japanese officer had written in our passports would pose a significant problem. Probably we would not be allowed by the customs of Egypt, a country in turmoil, to enter Egypt. This I had to avoid. While we were in the air I called a lawyer who I knew very well. I told him what had happened. He agreed to draft an official letter and to send it immediately to the customs of Cairo I hoped that this would do the trick.

The plane landed in Cairo and as expected we were picked up by the customs. We were taken apart again. Our passports were carefully studied. They said your photo doesn't look like you. I confirmed this and said it is an old picture. They also had already investigated if we were on the list of ICPO (International Criminal Police Organization). This was of course not the case. Another customs officer came with the official letter from my lawyer. Also this letter was studied closely. They asked Honey to take off her golden snake bracelet. She said it cannot be done. The customs than tried to remove the bracelet themselves but they didn't succeed. I did overhear them when they said we will follow her and cut off her arm. One of custom officers went away. I was sure that this custom officer would wait outside the airport on us and ambush us. After some discussion they decided to let us go. Due to our delay we were the only ones who entered the terminal. It was immediately clear that we were also there expected. Outside the terminal we hauled a taxi which sped away to Cairo. Cairo is Egypt's capital and the largest city in Africa. Due to the unbelievable traffic chaos and turmoil in Cairo we could not be followed. To be in Cairo is an overwhelming experience. More than 17 million people call it there home. It is smelly, dusty, chaotic, beautiful and has many museums. It is a city with ancient roots and exotic surroundings. Much can be seen in this metropolitan city which is located along the river Nile. In Cairo it was hot and humid.

Honey and I visited several museums in Egypt. I looked in the catalogs for artifacts related to Maat. However in none of the museums did I find an item that could be useful for your unique divine mission. I knew of course that it was atypical for a visitor to look for Maat. I had for many years been an archeologist in Egypt. I got strange glances from the conservators of

The Elevation to Divinity

the museums. This made me nervous I know how they operate. My search was however also noticed by a visitor. He followed us and when we were outside of one of the museums he addressed me. I am Abasi. Mr. Abasi asked if I was interested in Maat. I acknowledged this. Perhaps I have an artifact which could be of interest to you. I thought coincidence doesn't exist. Please follow me and get into my car. The artifact is in my house. I seriously doubted if this was a smart thing to do. But I also knew that it was important to find the special object for you my beloved Goddess Ira.

We left Cairo and drove higher up on the eastern bank of the Nile. After some time we saw a little village, or small group of huts with a cluster of palms and other trees. A little further on there was a narrow strip of cultivated land. A few miles further and we arrived in a small town where the houses were made of crude brick. Mr. Abasi stopped at one of these houses and said we were at his house. He brought us immediately to the cellar. Under the cellar was a grave. We entered the grave with respect. Mr. Abasi put on the flashlight and he showed us an astonishing painting of Maat and her daughter. On this painting, a young nude Goddess Ira was depicted. As far as I could judge it is an accurate representation of her when she was younger. I have seen photos from Goddess Ira when she was younger. It resembled her as closely as possible.

The painting of Maat and her daughter could be described as a natural painting. It was a good one, though slightly discolored with age, since I could easily recognize the beautiful curves and other details of you my Goddess. Around the painting there was a fine outline of a body which the daughter of Maat enclosed. I immediately had the feeling that this was the priceless artifact we searched for. I phoned you and told you of the painting on the wall of the grave. To be completely sure you had to visit the grave yourself. You send me a message that that you would take the first possible plane to Cairo.

And so you did. When I met you I took you with Mr. Abasi to the little town. There you saw the painting yourself and you knew immediately that this was the last item you had to collect. You hesitated if copying the painting would be adequate for your divine mission. Since you are a gifted artist you could do it yourself. It would also have been the easiest way. However after some deliberation you decided that copying was not good enough. You needed the real thing. The painting had to be chiseled out. You let Mr. Abasi know that you would like to buy the artifact. You asked him if this was possible and if it was legal. He answered both questions affirmative. He told us that the grave is under his house and that he as the owner of the ground and the building has the right to do as he sees fit. He picked the Egyptian legal code from the shelf and translated the relevant passage.

I must admit I personally had some doubts, but in the end we believed him when he said that buying the painting was legal according to Egyptian law. After some bargaining you agreed on the price. An important stipulation was that the price would only be paid if the painting could be chiseled out in one piece. Mr. Abasi then contacted a local contractor.

During the time we stayed in this little town the three of us would sleep in one of the rooms of his house. In this room, the guest room stood a twin bed. We were all tired. You put your body on the right side of the bed and I took the left side. But you became angry with me and said:" Property belongs on the ground. The left side of the bed is reserved for Honey." You put a leash on my collar and fixed it on one of the poles of the bed.

We took a lot of precautions to avoid damages and we were constantly present when they worked in the grave. First the contractor had to get behind the wall. It meant that the house had to be pillared. The building had to be maintained. After that the real work could begin. You instructed the contractor that the stone should be not too thick because it had to be exported. But it could also not be too thin otherwise the painting could fall to pieces and that should be avoided at all cost.

In the meantime when we were overseeing the work, Honey had rented a BMW. The rear seats of this car could be folded down. After the painting was chiseled out we put Styrofoam in the back of the car. It was a necessary precaution since the roads in Egypt are rather bumpy. On top of the stone we put some blankets and off we went. It was our intention that the stone would be shipped from Alexandria to Mexico.

We had an uneventful trip to Alexandria. When we arrived at the port of Alexandria we said goodbye to Honey and you released me from my ties with her. She would leave immediately to her homeland. I was not any longer her personal whore. As a reward for her services rendered she could keep the golden snake bracelet. After we had said goodbye I went away to get us some coffee. When I came back I saw that you were held in custody by the local authorities. Behind you stood a broad-chested guard with a long black truncheon in his hand. You ignored me completely and from that I understood that I had to stay in the background. From a distance I followed you. They brought you to one of the local police stations and I took a room across the street. Sometimes I was able to see you from there.

I had to have a new passport because my identity had changed and because of all the persons who sought me. I came into contact with a person who made false identity papers. He did a good job and I paid him with some of the golden coins I had received from Eeshain.

In the police station I Goddess Ira had not the routine preliminary interrogation to which nearly all prisoners were subject in Egypt. Even before the interrogation started the official authorities released a press statement. In this official statement they accused me and my accomplices of art theft and murder during a BDSM session. After my detention I saw that this press release was copied in all the important international newspapers. They made pretty juicy stories out of it. Some of them even published a picture of me as Mistress Lucrezia in one of my cat suits. Sometimes even with a whip in my hand.

There was a long range of crimes, not only art theft and murder, to which I had to confess. The confession in Egypt when art theft is involved itself is mostly just a formality. But the mental and sometimes physical torture was real. My interrogators were male as well as female. There were always four or five men in the room. They worked in shifts over periods that lasted ten or twelve hours at a stretch.

These interrogators saw to it that I was in constant discomfort. They tried to make me eat things I never do; they wrung my ears, they made me strip and searched me after each time I had left my room, ignored me when I had an asthma attack and refused me to leave the room to urinate. They also shone glaring lights in my face and gave me tranquilizers. But that was not all. Several times they put me in solitary confinement for at least 12 hours. The aim was to humiliate me and to destroy my power of arguing and reasoning. They asked me where my partners were. However to betray Honey or Osiris went against the core of my being. I had promised Osiris to protect him at all cost in the ownership agreement. I could not and would not violate this stipulation even if it would mean madness or the end of my life. I knew that Honey had already left the country but it was better that I took alone all the blame. Only Mr. Abasi had seen Osiris. Due to his change in appearance in Japan and his new passport he would not be found.

I quite often was handcuffed and beaten. They strip-searched me and photographed me while I was naked and subjected me tot electric shock and threaded to charge me with prostitution. I also was submitted regularly to "virginity tests "to degrade me further. When they were humiliating me they allowed men to watch and photograph what was happening and threaded to publicize those photographs.

Their real weapon however was the merciless questioning that went on and on hour after hour. Twisting everything I had said, convicting me at every step of lies and self contradictions until I began weeping as much of shame as nervous fatigue and then leaking wrong stories to the press and forcing me to watch television so I could witness the public opinion turning completely against me.

That did not give me reason to doubt my divine mission. I knew I was being tested but still there were times that I saw questions appearing in my head...Was it my delusion that I was a Goddess? Was it my task to save the world? Had I all imagined it? Had I really heard THE VOICE? Had I been in Japan? Was there even an Osiris? Or even if there was an Osiris had he played with me? As I never used tranquillizers before I couldn't even recognize the person I saw in the mirror when they allowed me, only once a week, to have a shower, cold water and a piece of soap, no shampoo or conditioner, no day or night crème. It made me feel very rough. After a few days I managed to hide the drugs they were giving me and at night I flushed them through the toilet so I had a clear head again and could start thinking about how I could get out of here. I hoped that Osiris would have established contact with Charlotte so my family could get involved and plead with the embassy.

The interrogators made reconstructions of what I had done. These reconstructions went like this: imagine that you are in the cellar with your accomplice making the deal with Mr. Abasi. Part of the deal was that you would give him a BDSM session after he had delivered the valuable artifact of which he claimed to be the owner. They confronted me with the local contractor. He confirmed the story the authorities had presented. He said that when he was about to leave, I was engaged in starting the BDSM session that was spoken for and that supposedly had taken place, and during that session Mr. Abasi should have died.

But there had never been a session programmed as part of the deal. I and Osiris had been parties in the deal but we paid as we had agreed on, with certificate for transportation stating I was now the rightful owner. Here they were now trying to pin murder on me saying I tortured him into signing the documents and that he lost his life due to the effects of the torture.

I demanded that his body would be examined for traces of violence or abuse, but they said his family did not want the body examined. I was so pleased when a guard came to fetch me cos I had a visitor. It was Charlotte, she looked very reassuring, and she said she had prepared my defense and was in contact with my lawyer and had a lot of people helping her to get me out. She said you are loved so much more than you can imagine. She never looked so sure of herself. She stated: I WILL get you out of here, at ALL costs.

In a way that gave me more confidence, I know how we can get once we bite into something.

When I returned to my cell they had planted another woman with me in my cell, she was Norwegian. She had been locked up wrongly accused as well, she was separated from her family and they were not informed that she was in their custody, she was refused a phone call and she was worried sick.

I tried to reassure her that things would fall in place and motivated her to be strong. She asked me so many questions that I lost my trust in her and thought they had planted her in my cell so I would confide in her.

I told her I was set up and accused falsely about something that is a forbidden act to their standards and I could end up being stoned in the square … The idea itself made me laugh and it surprised her I could joke about a thing like that.

Two days later Charlotte came to visit me again. I knew the cabins where we could speak behind glass were being monitored and listened into so we used our body language and an occasional dialect word so they could not follow what we were saying. I had also managed to write a message in the palm of my hand: NO OSIRIS I was alone.

Although I knew I was innocent and had not killed anyone, fact was that I had the artifact and that the person who, as it seemed wasn't the owner, had sold it to me was no longer alive to confirm my story. So beside the murder charge there was still also that art theft charge I had to deal with.

But it was better that I got charged alone, it would keep Osiris free, his privacy would not be endangered and he could do more outside the prison walls than to be locked up inside here with me, there was the mission that he had to complete and there was also Honey to think about. I was the only person able to establish contact with her and I had not informed Osiris yet about the precautions I had taken for the future and where he had to find all of that information. Also regarding to the privacy of Osiris I had made promises in the ownership agreement. I could not violate that trust although I knew that Osiris would let my interest prevail. I knew Charlotte had understood not to contact him for the time being as after her visiting me I was sure her phone was being monitored as well, same for the phones at the hotel she was staying. She said that she had the feeling that she was being followed and I am very sure that was the case.

She had constant contact with my lawyer, who tried to come as soon as he could get away. He said I did not make his life very easy by being wrongly accused 6 hours flying away. However he had found out that Mr. Abasi had been in poor health and that he had a criminal background. He probably got so stressed by the fear of being caught out by the authorities that he died of a heart attack. My lawyer also found out that Mr. Abasi died a few hours after I and Osiris had already left. But the police didn't believe him or they just did not want to believe him. They were so pleased with all the attention they were getting and the big case that caught all newspaper that they were completely blind for the truth. It seemed that not loosing face was more important than me losing my freedom and perhaps a lot more as well.

My lawyer was not allowed to visit me and to support me during the interrogations; they said it was not tolerated by their religion to leave a man with a woman alone in the same room when they are not married. I knew they were just trying to break me so I told Charlotte that my lawyer had to appeal for bringing my case in front of an international jury. That would mean that I had to be deported to a neutral country somewhere in the world. Art theft is a serious crime in Egypt. When they learned about my plans they tried to break me even more. If they could only get me to confess ASAP and have it over with.

Because of the press release and the death of Mr. Abasi, I received also a lot of death threats. To put me under pressure, they let me read these hate letters. This put almost unbearable pressure on me. The interrogators screamed abuse at me and threatened me most of the time. I had serious asthma attracts and during these attacks I could hardly breathe. Quite often I thought that I would choke.

How many times I had been interrogated I don't recall any more. There were times that I wanted my nerves to forsake me when I had to listen to the screams and howls of the Norwegian woman who they said would never see her husband and children alive again. They wanted to drive me mad. By divine providence this did not happen and I pretended to be under the influence of their drugs but in reality I took in all they said and started understanding their language. These interrogations, were, without being drugged, almost enough to make me put forth a confession of real and imaginary crimes. I went along with this madness game. I sometimes couldn't believe this was really happening it made me just want to have it over with. At other times I started out with the resolve of confessing nothing but there were also times I tried to make compromises. However when I was alone again I knew that the only way to get out of here was to stay strong, try to

The Elevation to Divinity

fit in, try to get as much sleep as possible and read all the time I had the opportunity.

I slept to make them believe I was under narcosis and I pretended that I had lost interest in their interrogations and that I accepted my faith as long as I could just get my drugs ...

That diagnosis of madness is what the authorities did not want to leak to the newspapers so when Charlotte wanted to visit me they told her I was too ill to see anyone.

I had of course suffered major allergic reactions to the food and I had lost so much weight that even my prizewinning arse had lost its lovely curves. When I looked at myself I knew I had lost my power of seduction and it would be harder to fight my way out. I had to rely upon the power of seduction I had passed on to my daughter Charlotte, but why did she no longer come to visit me?

After one of my allergic reactions I passed out and I seemed to have been talking a lot of nonsense, so they hired a local psychiatrist. But the psychiatrist made me only more confused.

Sometimes there were periods of recovery then they brought me to my cell. In my cell were two plank beds and a thin wash-basin, we had to share; they had also given us a bucket to pee in, as a kind of kindness. I hadn't been able to let anything pass through my colon, I felt blocked up and locked up, whilst the Norwegian woman suffered from the opposite

All interrogations were done with at least three persons present, one of them was a woman, she sometimes had to inspect me physically as I had used the right not to be touched by men as agreed on the Geneva convention. I knew that weeks ago I must have been a hot chick in their eyes but now I was a skeleton on flipflops with a worn-out coat and hair that klitted because of the sharp soap and the lack of conditioner, my skin felt like a piece of concrete, so dry.

When I was fetched again from my cell I was surprised that there was only one person in the room. Still having the reflections of what I had turned into these past few weeks in my head I assumed that to him I was no longer even considered a woman.

It was one of the inspectors who was very well informed about art and history and knew all about archeology of his country, he said he arranged this eye to eye contact because I was not a beast but a human being after all. I smiled by that remark and said: convince me of that then, that made him blush and it made me laugh as I suddenly felt like a woman or even just a person again.

Meanwhile my lawyer stayed in contact with Charlotte and they applied for international justice in a neutral country. From my home country they received a certificate of good conduct. The original was sent to Charlotte and she managed to give this certificate of good conduct to this inspector, as she felt that he was the only one that could be trusted. The certificate had been translated and an apostille was fixed on the translation.

We did not know if it would help but we were assured it had arrived at its destination in the right hands. The inspector also signed a note for Charlotte to have the right to visit me daily so Charlotte booked the same hotel across the street where also Osiris stayed.

All further interrogations were conducted in a friendlier manner and always by the same inspector. I started confiding in him and told him about my life as a Dominatrix and my elevation to divinity and how I wanted to make a difference in protecting the earth from existing, only by making people become aware of their being and its significance in the circle of life. The interrogations tuned into conversations, discussions, debates and I started looking forward to being fetched from my cell. He had ordered a few books for my from Rupert Sheldrake and in return I would explain him more about the phenomenon as his English wasn't bad but not of that kind to understand the way Rupert's thoughts are printed on paper.

I taught him how he could train himself to be aware of his receptors for picking up on those fields of knowledge or awareness by letting him perform tests at home. He got really interested in me as a person, not a sex symbol or a Diva. That made me think of when I was young and fought to be recognized for my brain, not my arse or pretty face.

In prison all that seemed significant in life just starts to seem trivial. And I had reflections of how I could have done things differently and where I had wronged people in the rush of my life, rushing to feel a rush all the time, never just being on the road but always focused on the destination.

I started writing down my thoughts and I found a kind of Zen over these miserable times. Miserable times I could not compare to anything as severe as the one I was in now.

Every time I caught a glimpse of the outside world I realized how important freedom is, what a fortune it is to be in good health and to have the possibility to be creative.

During one of the interrogations with this inspector he told me he got a vision just before he fell asleep. His vision was so real and insistent that he started to believe me. In his vision he had seen me drawn in a lot of money and he was a Maya that had just died and was on his way to the nebulah in a light bubble floating towards the heavens when he suddenly looked down to mother earth where he saw a river that turned into money. From this river of money I was trying to climb out but a foot stepped on my hand that was reaching for the edge. His bubble burst as if he had been shaken up to come to my rescue, he fell back to the earth into the river of money and when he landed the money turned into water again and there was no longer someone preventing me from climbing out.

He understood that it was he who was the man on the edge not reaching out to help me but to keep me struggling even though there was enough evidence for my innocence. He saw himself in the bubble because he was filled with proudness of having solved this big international case that made his miserable being a shining star. He said the answer lies in the money, there was a cash transaction. This the contractor acknowledged but the money was not found on the dead person or on me.

As the report of the autopsy had not come through, or perhaps hadn't even been conducted which could show the result of a heart attack he thought it likely that the contractor had taken the money when he found the old man dead and invented the story never even mentioning the money. Why else would he have lied about the BDSM session, cos he knew it would all blind us with disgust as much as it would make us curious. He admitted to me that he had arranged these private talks with me just because BDSM stories used to turn him on but now they seemed to have a different effect on him as we talked more. It was like his brain got stimulated into a more active, imaginative way of thinking and then they changed into conversations of pure knowledge that surrounded him and that he wasn't even aware of.

He said he had great admiration for me but that we were facing an almost impossible task to get me out of that situation. He also confided in me that he had erased the part of the recording where I and Charlotte are talking about bringing our case into international court. He said he did not know why he erased it. He also felt that the other investigators did not have to know I was still able to think clear. And he even confessed to me that he felt much smarter than his colleagues and that he thought he would have a better chance with me for getting my confession once I would have opened up to him . But after his vision he suddenly sees life in another perspective, he feels he wants to live instead of spending his life in prison, in darkness and unhappiness.

He had had his vision just at the time that I had given up all hope and was convinced that I had been led by delusions. That nothing of what had happened had been real at all and that I had committed the crimes. In spite of his training, this inspector was on my side now. He motivated me to stay with my beliefs and opinions. I do know you are the Goddess which we need against the wickedness here on earth.

At first I thought this is a trick to let me concede to the accused crimes or to give away withheld information, play the good guy, gain my trust, even flirt a bit in a way and of course playing the pupil. I thought that it was all a big conspiracy where they hire actors to play me. But slowly he was able to convince me of his good intentions. He told me about his lifestyle and that he was married and had two children but that he had married for the wrong reason. His children were very young compared to my Charlotte and I asked him why he started having children when he was nearly 40. He told me that when you reach the age of forty and are not married yet some families turn their back on you as the whole society considers you of being secretly gay. He said he never really fitted the pattern of most men as he was fascinated by the past and not the present, he would spend his time reading and visiting archeological sites and museums whilst his friends were dating girls so by the time his friends got wives the only thing he got were reading glasses. When he turned thirty he signed up for university studies in history just to get away from the narrow-mindedness of his family and to meet with more international students.

There he met an Iranian student, his family disapproved but he was blinded by his own aversion towards his family that he asked her to marry him just to prove them wrong. And how wrong he seemed to have been for that matter, cos the sweet, lovely, open minded and controversial girl he met at university turned into a religious tiran as soon as they had their first baby. His life had turned into a nightmare. But he said it was his own prison and coming to work was less of a prison than his home.

She hated the books he read, she was against all the things that had attracted him in her at the first place. She said she had taken it up as her mission to save his soul and had been deceiving him from the start as she was also convinced he had impure thoughts, she said she hated him for having gone down on her and the penetration of her anus but she said she did it all for the good cause so she could in the end make him aware of the filth he is spreading.

I was stunned when I heard this story, if he is inventing this to gain my trust I must say he is a sick mind, cos he was in tears and he said he had been living in shame ever since she told him the truth, he apologized for having used me to hear my stories and for not telling the truth when he admitted wanting to hear them, but that for him it was a way to become aware of

The Elevation to Divinity

not being a repulsive pervert because he wanted his wife to have an orgasm without the intention to conceive a child. He said that after the fight they had then they never even touched each other again. They still sleep in the same bed but he said he never felt as alone as he felt when he had to share the bed from that day on. Due to his unhappy marriage he signed up for almost every nightshift which started people gossiping about him raping inmates up there arse, his own wife being the source of that so that his family would break with him and choose her side and therefore the side of his offspring.

I said I've heard enough and that I would put my trust in him and I said that if he was double crossing me that he just had to live with the idea of being a good actor but a very bad human being.

He then hired a good local lawyer; together they were able to persuade his fellow investigators to examine the body of Mr. Abasi. Mr. Abasi was still in the fridge. A coroner did investigate the heart of the deceased. His findings showed that it was a miracle that Mr. Abasi had lived as long as he had already. There were also no traces of a BDSM session whatsoever. Thanks to this investigation the local authorities had to drop the murder charge.

The inspector confronted the contractor about stealing the money and said he would not give him away if he would withdraw his accusations against me and admit haven given a false testimony driven by his hatred towards all that came from the west.

But the crime charge of the art theft prevailed. In the meantime the inspector was convinced of his new vision. He told me that in his vision he saw that I had to find the center of the earth, the tree of life that was hidden when Adam and Eve ate from the tree of knowledge. He said in his vision there is a dagger that when pointed to the sun at the right time of day when the sun is at the same place as the nebulah is when it shows itself, I should be able to see the sun showing a map through the holes of the handle of the dagger. He told me that the dagger is to be found with a shaman in Hacienda Chitchen in Chichen Itza and a woman of wisdom uses it to bless people who come to seek a new vision for a new existence. So I had to go to Mexico, no matter what. That I had already heard from Dewi. He said he knew that I needed the artifact to complete my mission and gave me a business card of the Hacienda I should visit and the woman I should ask for. He promised to help me smuggle the artifact out of the country by letting a deputy bring it to the museum and be a victim to an attack for the artifact, it would then be transported to Amsterdam, from where it would be shipped as a piece of a Maya temple to Mexico. He assured me it would arrive at the destination before I would and that it would be in good hands. The less I knew the better.

He knew he took a big risk in doing this and was quite sure that it would not take very long before the others realized he has changed sides but he had made up his mind that he was going to quit his job anyway and start a new life elsewhere..

I was lucky that after some time the local authorities decided that I had been punished enough by the international media attention. However I had to pay a heavy bail and was not allowed leaving Cairo. Osiris had given Charlotte the golden coins form Eeshain, these I used to pay the bail. After another eleven days the local authorities released me. Luckily for me the inspector kept his word and helped me. He managed to smuggle me out of Egypt to Turkey and before I knew it I was at the airport of Istanbul booking my flight to my homeland and from there I would book a touristic holiday to Mexico. The stone, the inspector assured me will be on his way before the authorities realize I have vanished.

Osiris had also arrived home again. His wife believed him that he had been on a very long business trip and that he got involved in an archeological experiment which cut him off from the civilized world. Osiris told me that he could not avoid to full filling his marital duties the first night he was home. The ownership agreement allowed this. He told me that the bed room was very dark when the intercourse took place. It was simple straightforward. The tattooed penis went up and down into her hairless vagina and in a few minutes it was over. It was strange he told me. It was the first time that his wife had fucked the tattooed penis. He was confused since he had ceded his penis to me. Was it him or was it me who fucked his wife. He had become so conditioned and his thoughts and feelings had become almost hundred percent my thoughts and feelings that during this short intercourse with her he thought that I had intercourse with her. It is an ecstatic feeling when you realize that your mind control is so absolute.

The Elevation to Divinity

Artistic Goddess Ira saved the world.

7 Sophisticated Goddess Ira

When I arrived home, I found a coded instruction from the Japanese tattooist Kioshi. It said:"let Charlotte take the stone box to... in Mexico. There is a temple, a hidden temple, that holds the final key, contact Hacienda Chichen, book a room there for a few days, once there you will meet the elder heeler, you will recognize her as soon as you talk to her, in fact, it will be she who will recognize you both, she will address Charlotte first, as her future lies in Mexico, so did her previous lives, she will be needed as a part of the deal, they will need her. Let Osiris follow later; pretend you and your daughter are enjoying a spiritual holiday.

Osiris must plan his trip separately and take rooms at different hotels, only meet by accident, don't travel together, use a personalized chat Application for the iphone and erase all communication history, from now on: no sms, phone or mail contact, you are being monitored, don't speak in your house about your plans, divert those who are monitoring by feeding them wrong information.

Leave immediately else you will be too late for the conclusion of your divine mission.

I booked a flight for the next morning at 6 am. I asked Charlotte to arrange a ride to the airport separate from me in case something went wrong. One of her contacts would arrange new identity papers for both of us. I was now Angela and Charlotte was Lolita. I had told her not to pack too much so we would be a pair of typical yoga tourists.

I had booked a holiday of 4 weeks as had been advised to be able to fulfill my quest but for Charlotte I had booked an open ticket so she could finalize the work after I had left the country. I took with me the secret scroll of Dewi to show to the elder heeler once I would arrive in Hacienda, but that was only my 3rd destination to avoid giving away my identity and intentions.

I packed the scroll between some books about morphic resonance and tattoos of the Mayas and a book symbols throughout the centuries.

I used a comfortable shiny black suitcase that had a separate lockable system, so no unauthorized opening would be possible. As hand luggage I took stewards hand luggage on wheels where I had all booking references and my laptop, chargers and iphones. Separately attached on my suitcase were four variations of yoga mats so it would look like the goal of my visit, apart from visiting temples.

As I could not find any yogi activity in the Hacienda it was almost opposite one of the most famous temples "Chichen Itza" and they had a very good spa with sjahman rituals and sacred grounds and a cenote for blessings.

Our journey would start in a 4 day yoga inspired eco hotel at Isla Mujeres, Na Balam Suites Beach hotel, followed by a 3 day intensive yoga workshop in Tulum, at another ecohotel called Playa Azul, from there I would visit the temple ruins of Tulum and would take a guided tour to Chichen Itza and stay there for 4 days, where after we would meet up with Osiris who we would meet in Merida, where he will be booked into a hotel and where we spent the day shopping. We had arranged to meet on the market at 10 am after 12 days (We would come to his rescue when someone tries to rip him of when he wants to buy a skull for his wife).

After that encounter we would stay in the area for 10 days where we reserved some private dorms in Palenque and Merida so we could move around as we pleased without losing too much money and to end the holiday we would take up yoga again at isla Holbox where we booked lodgings and spa and yoga in Casa del Tortugas. I would then take the flight back from Cancun after exactly 28 days as you need to on chartered flights.

When I left for the airport I noticed that a car seemed to follow me, it was 3 am in the morning so the highway was almost empty and I was sure he was parked at the park and ride near to where I live. This gave me an uneasy feeling. At the airport I walked around on my own for some time, as I had seen Charlotte still being in company, so they were still dealing with the identity papers. As agreed and according to the pictures on the new ID papers I had cut my hair in an asymmetrical bob, which was hidden under a baseball cap now.

Charlotte had died her hair red, same color as her red lips. Her suitcase was red, all the content in it was red and she of course wore red shoes and red dress.

I wore my black dance shoes as they have no metal inside, back dance pants and matching short top. With my tattoo inspired by the Maya culture on my belly visible for all of them too see, there would be nothing suspicious to our holiday.

When I saw the guy leave from the table where Charlotte was drinking tea, I knew she had succeeded in her part of the preparations and as I had already described she was all in red, handbag included.

I joined her for breakfast and we had an easy check-in with the false identity papers, I knew that there was an extradition treaty between Egypt and Mexico (more for object than for people, but why take risks?)

By signed letter I had given Osiris the instructions to go to Merida, he would take the ADO bus from Cancun airport and to book a room in hotel Casa del Balam. When he would arrive in Mexico was of no importance, only that he would meet me 12 days later at the market, around the corner of his hotel. If one of us could not make this appointment we would try the same time and same place for 4 days before we would go over to plan B, a plan that was the backup plan in case one of us would not have been able to make it to this point.

Because Osiris had changed significantly and was provided with a false passport it was not difficult for him to fly to Mexico without being noticed.

Charlotte and I arrived in the afternoon local time in Cancun and the tour operator had organized the transport to Isla Mujeres. The hotel, Na Balam Suites, was a very nice and spacious eco bungalow directly on the white sandy beach under palm trees. In the morning we did our yoga training, Yin Yoga Stretch, which is calm and all about the stretch in your body, with peaceful music, in your own time followed by meditation, given by a German woman, who had been living on the island for 20 years. She gave us some tips and more information on the history of the island and offered to take us to the ruins of the temple where the island got its name from: Isla Mujeres is woman island, at the ruins it's the place in Mexico where you can be the first to see the sun rise, women used to go to the temple when they were getting married or with child for either fertile blessing or a blessed birth .

There was only little left from the temple but the surroundings were so beautiful. As she had been living on the island for so many years she could get things done, and we could visit the place after tourist hours, it was the same when we went for drinks after, tequila with scorpion inside, white mescal, frozen tequila, if it was a specialty on the island, she would get it for us. Charlotte started collecting skulls and the days passed with yoga, food, beach, shopping, restaurant and late drinks at the local bar.

We almost forgot about the stress situation I had been in just 2 weeks ago. 4 days later we booked the transport from Isla Mujeres to Tulum via the tour operator with an included excursion to visit the temple of Chichen Itza

We arrived at this very nice little town, so different from Cancun and on the same stretch of the coastline of Quintana Roo, all big fancy hotel chains had disappeared and we seemed to have arrived at a part of non-tourist Yucatan, which after a while we learned was not true either, but it was certainly the place for yoga and relaxation. We signed into our hotel Playa Azul, where we had a very lovely cabana for 2 persons with a huge bed in the middle covered by a big mosquito net. I had been warned for that place and mosquitoes but I had already suffered an allergic reaction at Isla Mujeres. The people in the hotel were absolutely delightful and we joined in with the morning yoga that was given in the place next door at the Bikini Bootcamp.

We had long talks and long walks along the coastline and watched the kite surfers or had a drink at the hotel beach bar or in the evening at the Mezcal Bar in the town center. Tulum had a different kind of tourism, certainly lots of yogi, but also lots of students, tattoo artists, musicians, artists and all hotels were set up with cabanas and they were all eco-minded. The water from the shower came out of two shells that joined in the middle, cold and hot, yin and yan.

The hotel had a spa and we both enjoyed an amazing treatment given by a girl who lives in the mountain in the north of Mexico. She told me about old rituals and wrappings and the center of the woman and that she personalized the treatment she gave me to the energy she felt coming from me and with that energy she would start her treatment so that I would be a complete part of it. Her English was rather well so I was sure I had not misunderstood her.

She said she only used herbs and fruits and aromas that are found everywhere and in their original shape. She scrubbed me with the remainders of freshly made coffee, she covered me with papaya juice, which she squeezed out of ripe papayas, she used yoghurt and she used some sacred words when she let me smell different scents. After more than an hour I could suddenly feel my body lifting itself with a lightness I had never known before, hardly surprising when I realize I am still on the table and the other me is standing, over better floating, over the coastline staring into the endless beauty I had gazed upon only this morning. I had left my body, it filled me with delight and I had never felt this lightness of being. After a while I re-joined my mortal shape again and the treatment continued with a kind of local clay covered by big banana leaves that was all over my body. I was in very deep relaxation and after I was washed from the clay I received an hour long oil massage in which I could recognize eucalyptus, lavender but there was a lot more …This was certainly the best treatment I had got in my entire life.

They are quite good in Mexico for things like that; usually we think that the Thai people or Chinese are the experts. I certainly had two blissful ones in Tulum. The second one was the next day when I had a deep tissue one in town and I can assure you, he went really deep! So deep that his wife got really jealous. Those two and "the treatments for the gods" I once had in Munich in a Turkish hammam!

The next day we started the day with our ashtanga yoga. Ashtanga yoga is a system of yoga transmitted to the modern world by Sri K. Pattabhi Jois (1915-2009). This method of yoga involves synchronizing the breath with a progressive series of postures—a process producing intense internal heat and a profuse, purifying sweat that detoxifies muscles and organs. The result is improved circulation, a light and strong body, and a calm mind.

We learned how to open and close with mantras:

Ashtanga opening mantra:
vande gurunam charanaravinde, sandarsita svatmasukhava bodhe
nihsreyase jangalikayamane, samsara halahala mohasantyai
abahu purusakaram, sankhacakrasi dharinam
sahasra sirasam svetam, pranamami patanjalim
om

I bow to the lotus feet of the guru who awakens insight into the happiness of pure Being, who is the final refuge, the jungle physician, who eliminates the delusion caused by the poisonous herb of samsara [conditioned existence]. I prostrate before the sage Patanjali who has thousands of radiant, white heads [in his form as the divine serpent, Ananta] and who has, as far as his arms, assumed the form of a man holding a conch shell [divine sound], a wheel [discus of light, representing infinite time] and a sword [discrimination].

Ashtanga mangala closing mantra:

The Elevation to Divinity

om
svasti prajabhyam paripalayantham nyayeana margena mahim maheesah
gobrahmanebhya shubamsthu nityam lokah samastha sukhino bhavanthu
om
om shanti, shanti, shantihi

May there be well being to the people
May the kings rule the earth along the right path
May the cattle and the Brahmins have well being forever
May all the beings in all the worlds become happy
Peace, peace and peace be everywhere!

Between those two mantras we did our practice, of the different salutations to the Sun, nonstop for 60 mins long.

The rest of the day was spent lazing at the beach and at 3 pm we visited the Tulum ruins and good we did as they close at 6 pm. It was very busy and full of American tourists. We looked around, took pictures and I used my camera in search for some hidden sign but I did not pick up on something like that. It was a pretty site but for me it didn't really "do" anything.

Early on the next morning we had an excursion booked to the temple of Chichen Itza. I had hidden the scroll in my camera bag and just like all tourists I wanted to video the temple.

I reality my video camera had been slightly adjusted to be able to see what others couldn't see, it doesn't only have night shot mode on it, it also has a deep infrared function on it that can go through substances of organic matter. You don't see it on the camera; it is a sort of extra battery I attach where this function has been built in.

It seemed ideal for trying to find a hidden temple. I felt quite nervous to have the scroll and the camera in one and the same bag so I asked Charlotte if she could hide the scroll upon her person until lunchtime, where we had booked lunch at the Hacienda.

The temple visit was early in the morning, as the tour operator had advised to leave Tulum around 7 am to avoid too many tourists because it is usually very busy from 11am onwards.

They said we could also attend an evening event at the temple, but I said we would decide about that later, or even if we wanted to stay longer we would just call the tour operator and change the plans. He had given me his business card just to be sure.

It was immense and impressive, our private guide told us about the history of the temple and the rituals and the snake that you can see descending and also the difference in sounds when you shout to the temple, changing when you are north, south, east or west, which we of course had to test ourselves. The temple and the stories around it were so much more inspiring then the visit to the Tulum ruins, although the very small ruins at Isla Mujeres also had that magical, inspiring feeling about them.

Looking back on that I was so grateful we had the change to visit at least one of them without tourists and sales people, throwing wooden carvings and small temples around your head.

The guide was very well informed and he told us many stories about the Mayas and their rituals and their knowledge and how they were the first people that could count, so we learned all about the Maya calendar and that the whole Maya culture was based on nature, they live off, for and from, but they showed grace and gave nature what it wanted in return, respect, not abuse.

After 2 hours I thanked our private guide with a handful of dollars and said I would enjoy just walking around on my own a bit, he could however still show Charlotte more of it and explain her more about the history. I then took my camera and started filming everything, the whole surroundings of the temple, from every angle, the big place full of colons, the huge square that seemed endless and the very steep cenote. A cenote is a kind of sinkhole with exposed rocky edges containing groundwater. Then I suddenly saw an unfinished temple. It looked a bit like a sacred offering place, I move closer towards it and I can enter without anyone telling me not to, unlike the temple and the 1000 collon gallery. But when I look around me I see I am all alone, following my camera I had not paid attention to where I was actually going and what was happening around me.

The place looked like an altar when I climbed on it I felt the presence of a very strong spirit, it kind of seemed to lead me to the center of it and before I realized I was standing on a high piece of stone my arms raised to the sky as if I was trying to let go or receive something. I was blinded by the sunlight and I must have been in a beam of sunlight at that precise moment. When I realized I had been staring in the sun I averted my eyes to the floor and there I saw the words: YAXKIN. I was in the center of a sanctuary of Life!

After a few moments I realized I had left my camera on one of the pillars in front of this sanctuary to be able to have a total view of it all, and yes, it was still running, I rewinded it back about 10 mins and there I saw that what had just happened was not a segment of my imagination, it was real, I had experienced something unique, on the video I am completely taken by the light as if I am captured in a sunbeam, but I have no burn marks and also my eyes don't feel as if they have been staring in the brightest sun ever, as I can see very clear.

Something had happened to my inner-self, not my body, my inner-self feels like it is on fire without the burning feeling; I just have to go the Hacienda. As I have no idea where I had gone to, I just followed my instinct and arrived flawless at the Hacienda in no time.

Time had stood still or I had forgotten it existed, and I saw Charlotte waiting for me at the restaurant area, trying to gain access with her phone to the internet. It surprised me it was 1pm already. Charlotte asked me what had happened to me as I looked like I had met or turned into a ghost, she also said that the elder heeler from this place has already spoken to her, she had said to her:" your future is near and it lies there where we have not gained access yet, we have been waiting for you, we will see each other again soon and I will explain, thereafter we will always be joined."

She said the woman was so friendly and she had so much energy that she had no doubt at all about the words she had just heard, Charlotte had found her guide, she had her own personal quest in Mexico, she was looking for answers she could not find, she wanted to learn where reality and subconscious join or part and where one can alter them to your own needs or desirers.

We were both stunned by what had happened, but also aware of the danger that was also close to us as we felt the presence of the spirits and enlightenment so close, it never shows itself without demons or darkness close by, that darkness could come in any shape … so we decided we would talk about the events on a later time during the day and join in with the other people for the lunch and take the bus back to Tulum as we had booked it not to arise suspicion. We will, however pay a deposit for the room we have pre-booked for the day after tomorrow and I will ask if I can leave a few personal belongings like my camera behind in safe keeping as the second part of the tour would take us to a cenote in the jungle for swimming. I asked Charlotte for the scroll and hid it with the camera, which I've put on a lock for the film I had just made. They said they would keep it for me and were very pleased with the 500 dollar cash in advance for our stay. The man I spoke to introduced himself then and he said his name was Jose and he is the shaman from the Hacienda, he gave me a flyer with more information about the hotel, the Maya foundation and the spa, which was called, what else then: YAXKIN.

I had a feeling that neither the camera, nor the scroll would be safe on me, as I was not sure about the same people that we saw in Isla Mujeres, that were also in Tulum and now here at Hacienda, was that coincidence or were they observing?

In the bus to Ek Balam, the cenote, I hardly spoke a word about what had happened, we engaged into talking about our previous boyfriends and in what cases they had similarities and what we liked and disliked about them. In the cenote we could see the most beautiful colors and the freshness of the water was amazing, the sun would shine like pure gold, flirting with the water and a part of the wall of the cave, reflecting that light again to the opposite side of the cave... I was really sure now that nature hides her treasures as long as she can, pretty soon this sacred place will fall into the hands of a rich American project developer and they will build a wellness hotel around the cave. I felt like I was now part of this and it made me sad to think that I have missed so much beauty in my life because I was unable to see...

At that moment I also felt how powerful nature could be, as if she picked up my thoughts about wanting to protect her, it starting pouring with rain and there was a massive thunderstorm. I apologized whispering that she had made her point. It made me feel very small to be thought a lesson by mother earth this way, it left me a bit in doubts about my significance but by the time we had left the path leading to the bus, she had stopped showing off and the ride back to Tulum was a very peaceful one.

That night me and Charlotte sat at the beach all night and we talked about what had happened today and how we felt and how all that has happened before in our life's had seemed to have lead to this moment. We sat very close together at the waterside where the wind was playing with our hair a bit and the sand was just naughty enough to polish our finger and toenails and to find its way into our pants. We sat there all night, sharing a bottle of red wine, one of my favorites I had brought with me for a special occasion, Alter Ego from Chateau Palmer, couldn't think of a better time and place for it.

The next day passed slowly with some Easy-flow yoga instead of the asthanga yoga, as that's what they do on weekends. Strange that we had no sense of what day of the week we were at all, but did it matter at all in the first place, neither me nor Charlotte have really been living with the clock and a 9 to 5 job and holidays and weekends.

But we both couldn't wait until we could start our journey to Chichen Itza. That evening we went to the mescal bar where the bartender had offered that we could use his car as he wasn't using it at all himself. I kindly accepted his offer but gave him 250 dollars for it, if I didn't have to worry about what date I would bring it back, but it would be before my departure. He had no problem with that at all so we drove back to the hotel in the evening, parked the car just outside of the hotels zone and we walked back the last part. After morning yoga, which I attended alone as Charlotte had sore muscles, and breakfast we checked out and asked for a taxi, which only had to take us to the car nearby, so the other people in the hotel didn't know we now had our own wheels.

We were very excited about our journey, we were chatting away when suddenly we are stopped by the army, they had locked off the entire road and we were kindly asked to step out of the vehicle, some young officers came towards the car and Charlotte started flirting with them, which was not really appreciated by el commandante and the young officers were told off and we signaled to leave. I felt relieved and thanked Charlotte for being so creative, She replied: "I was really into that guy…his name is Eduardo, I am sure I will find him again". It made me think what could have happened if they would have found the scroll or the images on the camera.

About 2 and a half hours later we arrived at the Hacienda Chichen, were we were welcomed by Beatrize, the elder heeler, she said: "The princess and the queen have returned, welcome home, this place has missed you. We had been informed in a ritual that you were on the way, please come in and sit down, I will explain you everything".

She continued: "The Gods have been giving us signs that the new Maya princess was on her way here, we have been celebrating her birthday for the past 21 years, she who is born on 20th of December, she will return before 20th December 2012 to give us faith that the end of the world is not the end of life, she will teach us and we will open her and give her power and develop her abilities that are considered "abnormalities of disfunctions" in the world you come from where no-one listens to nature, where rules are made by people and not by nature, where nature is enslaved to the human tortures, drained from its energy sources, used and abused, tortured deeper into the layers where natural repair is almost impossible, without severe changes. There is so little time left to spread awareness, to fill hearts with love, the love for nature, instead of pockets with money. What is happening to nature is what has happened so many years ago to the Mayas, the worshippers of nature, we did not have the strength to fight back nor the resources, but we could have had natures help to destroy those who had destroyed us and our beliefs and our treasures. We did not want to as we never thought mankind would be so unworthy and unrespectful towards the greatest gift around us. Still up to today we hope for a miracle, a princess that will be the icon for love, dressed in red, the color of love and passion and blood. The queen who can be respected and believed in, people need a leader, but not a tiran, this time we have to do it all differently, we have prepared this since the beginning of time, when we hid the temple where we hid the tree of life, when the tree of knowledge was abused we hide our strength deep below the surface. You are the only ones who can have access, only the chosen ones. We need to be reassured. This evening we will start with our rituals. Are you willing to go through this process?"

We both said we were ready. Then we ate and we were lead around the premises and our bungalow." After the ritual it is important you go to sleep immediately, that is why your bungalow is next to the spa and the rituals are in the garden of your bungalow, it is build on the edge of sacred ground, you will feel the energy when you sleep, all the enlightenments you have had over the past years and more recent will all join in your sleep tonight, that's why it is important to sleep ", she then, turned to me saying:"I know it is difficult for you but during my ritual, me and my girls, will make sure we add the desire to sleep in your body, it will be in a bubble that will burst once you are comfortable in bed, use the bed on the right side of the wall." "We will see you at 6pm, I will now go and gather the necessary herbs for the ritual, and I need a few hours to prepare." Then she turned and took us both close to her, like a mother would do and said:"This is one of the happiest moments in my life, I can contribute with heart, soul, body and mind to what I see as the greatest mission of my life, I will free many souls and I will be a free one myself, we all will be...." And then she left.

We decided to take a rest at the side of the pool and then showered before we presented ourselves for the first "treatment"

We were introduced to the two other Mayan therapists and then submitted to the "Kukulcan" Maya God holistic Spa ceremony, which was rooted in holistic Maya ceremonies: Full body (earth and water), mind (fire) and spirit (air) alignment and energy treatment.

It's a supreme Maya spa therapy created to renew your spirit, clean and invigorate your body and restore the equilibrium and serenity of the mind, bringing into physical manifestation the true nature of your spirit, this holistic ritual will align the energies of earth, water, fire and air in you. Anointing the body with Xunan Kabroyal pure honey, delicately mixed in sacred Maya clay body wrap, the heater will unblock your energy flow with a gentle facial, aromatherapy, reflexology, Maya crystal and gemstone therapy.

We could feel these energies just like it was described, however we started the ritual with Maya blessings and we ended the ritual in presence of the Sjaman, who gave us a special gift that we received inside, we would know when it would be time to release it.

We then were taken outside and walked for a while until we came to the sacred grounds for meditation, the elder heeler, Beatrize, translated to us the Maya words to put us into meditation state so we could understand the words we were supposed to repeat after the sjaman... Pretty soon we were in a state of total openness. We sat there till midnight staring at the stars and feeling completely rejuvenated and open, very open ... Then Beatrize told us that we were now spending the rest of the night "Zumpul-che" in a Mayan Sacred cave and Sweat Bath, for Ancient Body, Mind and Spirit purification.

We were first anointed with essential oils and prepared with rhythmic sounds of mystic Caracol calls whilst each stone in the cava was carefully poured by special healing cenote water that was brewed with Mayan herbs. We were then left alone in the cave whilst outside Mayan singing and drums were played, we were seated on the wet stones and the cave was very hot, this cleansing ceremony has the natural, beneficial effects and purification properties of fire and water, as cosmic sources for personal healing to unblock the energy flow of spirit and the physical body. A few times during the night we had to leave the cave to pour ice-cold cenote water over us outside the cave to cool our bodies for further purification until it was 6 am and the sjaman and Beatrize brought us, wrapped in a towel to the meditation garden were we were given a specially brewed drink of mineral and herb infusions.

That had some kind of hallucinating effect on me. I saw myself, wrapped with a hip cloth walking into a temple, it seemed a familiar one to me as I went straight for the altar without any hesitation in my movements, there I opened a few hidden gates by placing the palm of my hand on the wall, to arrive at the altar where I opened a small coffin that was locked by a big lock with twenty-eight signs of the ancient letter type of hieroglyphs. I saw myself choosing the 4 correct ones and opened the coffin and found a very old golden dagger with stones in the handle.

I raised it high towards to Gods portrayed on the altar and with a bow

I left the place with the dagger which I wrapped in my hip cloth... I left the temple completely naked and went to an open space a few miles away from the temple and held the dagger towards the sun. It blacked out the sun and its light came through the dagger pointing at 3 different places far from where I was. It seemed like I fully understood what I was doing as I saw myself wrapping the dagger again into my cloth and I walked away, out of the bright sunshine until I saw myself standing in front of me, placing the dagger in my hands, whilst you walked back inside of me ... it took me a while before I came out of my hallucinating state, but when I came round I was still seated in the meditation garden in my towel, but I was holding this ancient relique in the form of a dagger, half wrapped by a piece of cloth, in my own hands.

I realized that this was the missing piece I was supposed to find at the Hacienda, how it had really been presented to me will probably stay a mystery forever, but I knew I had to wrap it into the cloth and hold it close to me, when I looked around me there was nobody there anymore, even Charlotte was gone. So I decided to fetch my bathrobe that was near the cave and where my key was to go back to my room immediately.

There were still 3 days before my scheduled meeting with Osiris in Merdia and I did not want to jeopardize that meeting from taking place but I had such a desire to let him know I had succeeded in my mission and had found what we were promised to find here.

I hid the dagger carefully in my suitcase into a small flat beauty-case and locked it. I pushed in my personal code on the lock and I saw a red flickering light on the side of the lock, I pulled out the ring of the lock and hung it on the neck jewel with the green stone Osiris had given me some time ago, the little green light on the inside of the ring was almost invisible that way, but was an assurance that the dagger was still at the place I had hidden it. There was no way I would leave things to chance.

The next days we continued our pleasant stay at the hacienda and we were further purified and blessed by other rituals "Yaxkin" a stress relief Maya ritual, "kakaw" an exquisite indulgence to celebrate life's joys, "pakal" to stimulate the senses and "Pepen" a ritual for grace and beauty and we ended with the "Su'uk – Goddess ritual "to regenerate the whole being.

Completely purified, blessed, rejuvenated and regenerated we said goodbye to Beatrize and the sjaman and the lovely people around her and we handed her an envelope that would help the Maya foundation with the good work they have been doing for the elders and the children of the Mayas in the area.

She thanked us with gifts that came from the heart and she gave Charlotte a very special heavy silver ring in the shape of a snake that bend 3 times around her finger. She said:"Wear this every day, then every day I will be with you ...." Charlotte was in tears and I knew that they had a special moment, one I was not part of.

She gave me her golden bracelet with the signs of the Maya calendar engraved in it, she said:"I am sure you have found what you were looking for, if you ever get lost in time or space this bracelet will help you find your way back." We hugged and then we left and walked out of the Hacienda towards the place I had left the car.

It was time to go to Merida where we were supposed to meet Osiris in less than 20 hours from now. It gave us time to check-in to the hostel, Nomades, we had prebooked. The locked beauty-case I hid in my camera bag, although our stuff in our private dorm was supposed to be safe I'd rather not leave it behind unattended.

We enjoyed a walk through the shopping streets and bought very nice dresses and had a very lovely dinner with a bottle of red wine near the hotel where I figured Osiris must have checked in by now. It was a very typical Mexican restaurant with some American western movie accents to it, it was spacious and nicely decorated and we were sitting outside where we had a total view over the market place and the entrance of the hotel as well.

However, we did not see Osiris going in, nor out, he was probably suffering from jetlag and resting in order not to miss our meeting tomorrow. Meanwhile Charlotte had a meeting with one of the army men that we ran into a few days ago, she said she had made contact with him through facebook.

We left at midnight and went back to the hostel. I enjoyed a good sleep after the red wine I had consumed. Charlotte, however decided to go elsewhere with the army guy she called Eduardo. She said: "trust me, I have a plan…"

The next morning at 9 am I saw Charlotte again at breakfast, she had a big parcel under her arm which she hid in a private locker, without questions asked we left for the market place again, with my camera bag locked under my arm, hoping to find Osiris.

We stopped at each stand at the market and acted like excited tourists shopping for souvenirs and looking to do some bargains. After at least an hour or so we saw a man that resembled Osiris, he was dressed in off-white cotton suit and wore a straw hat, but a kind of fancy one with a black ribbon around it and linen shoes, he was wearing brown sunglasses so from a distance I wasn't quite sure but I saw Charlotte had the same impression and walked straight towards him. She started discussing with the seller of the jewel Osiris was holding in his hand and told him that he shouldn't rip off tourists like that. Osiris lowered his glasses and thanked Charlotte in English for her help stating that his Spanish is a bit rusty, inviting her to have a drink with him.

She then signaled me to come and explained that this poor man was being robbed and she came to his rescue and he now kindly invited us for a drink. I accepted his kind offer and the three of us walked off to the place we had dinner the night before.

We had established contact in a non-suspicious way; we decided to speak about tourism and the temples and had the conversation entirely in English, where I sort of briefed him a bit about the content of our holiday mentioning the visit to the Hacienda as one of the highlights.

He then asked if we would be so kind as to escort him there as Chichen Itza was on his list of to visit temples and he had only arrived yesterday. When he said he wanted to rent a car we said we would gladly pick him up at his hotel the next morning and perhaps we would run into each other later as we were just spending the day shopping in Merida again.

We said goodbye and I asked him for his room number and a card from the hotel in case I would be running late the next morning. I then went to a Telcel shop and bought 2 phones with a prepaid amount of calling value and Mexican numbers. It would be easier to communicate that way.

From my hostel I called Osiris room at 7 am and told him I would pick him up at 8.30 precisely and that it would be easier if I could pick him up at the corner of the street.

He was waiting there for me so we drove off to Chichen Itza. I handed him the phone I had bought yesterday and explained to him that I had programmed it to talk and text to each other coded and because it were unregistered Mexican numbers our communication could not be picked up very easily. Of course I knew that the software I had downloaded the night before would be easily cracked by someone who is as good as I am with technology and high-tech toys, of all sorts.

I told him how I had acquired this car and that it was safe to talk but it was better to switch off all electronic devices so no-one could listen in on us. I told him about the rituals and how I had found the relique we were looking for and that I had to visit three places to find out which of them was the actual place we had to go. But I also said it might be possible to avoid this as we could perhaps repeat what I had seen in my hallucination, by being at the same spot and holding up the dagger towards the sun. I wasn't sure about the time in my hallucination but the sun seemed to be in the place where it is when I am in warrior pose (the pose that builds focus in my ashtanga yoga) which would mean it should be around 1pm. The only problem was that I couldn't really see the place very well, I could only remember how long it took to walk away from the temple towards it and that it was in the direction of the sun.

We arrived at 9.45 at the temple of Chichen Itza and Osiris was overwhelmed, I told him we would have time for a visit more closely later as we first had to find the place of my hallucination. He begged for half an hour which I granted him as it is quite spectacular. We then followed towards the direction of the sun; we had to start over about 3 or 4 times until I recognized a sculpture from my hallucination. This is the place we had to be, and the time was also near to the point, I went into warrior pose to focus and the sun was almost at the position in my hallucination. Osiris repeated my action to focus in the same way and I explained him why this pose is building focus. When we repeated the total sun Salutation he could feel a different energy floating around his body and before we realized we had arrived at the point where the sun was almost touching my hands.

It was time we held the dagger up and see if we could establish the place where we could commence our search for the hidden temple. We decided we would make a picture whilst I was holding the dagger in front of the sun. The three holes would be clearly visible. That way we could draw a map of the area in different scales, one that would be of Ycatan, another of Mexico, another of the ancient Maya region and another of the world. On all these maps we should always arrive at the same point if the prophecy was right and we had of course the guidelines that Kioshi had given us.

We decided that after Osiris had been able to have a look at the temple we would have dinner together at the Hacienda, where I introduced Osiris as someone who is like-minded and a true believer in the soul. He then had the pleasure of sharing some of Beatrize wisdom and her knowledge of the history of the Maya culture.

With a lot of enthusiasm she started explaining where the Maya's were situated and around what time and what traces they left behind and where they still are situated. "Unlike the cultures of the Valley of Mexico, the urban centers were only important for the Maya's during the Classic period from 300 to 900 AD. The culture of the Maya's, however, has little changed from the Classic period to the modern period, for Maya culture was largely tribal and rural all throughout the Classic period. What distinguishes

Classic from post-Classic Maya culture was the importance of urban centers and their structures in the religious life of the Mayas and the extent of literate culture.

The Mayas were never a "true" urban culture; the urban centers were almost entirely used as religious centers for the rural population surrounding them. Therefore, the decline of the urban centers after 900 AD did not involve titanic social change so much as religious change; it is believed by some scholars that the abandonment of the cities was primarily due to religious proselytizing from the north. Nevertheless, the Classic period saw an explosion of cultural creativity all throughout the region populated by the tribes we call "Mayan". They derived many cultural forms from the north, but also devised many cultural innovations that profoundly influenced all subsequent cultures throughout Mesoamerica. Much of Maya culture, particularly the religious reckoning of time, is still a vital aspect of Native American life in Guatemala and Honduras.

Classic Maya culture developed in three regions in Mesoamerica. By far the most important and most complete urban developments occurred in the lowlands in the "central region" of southern Guatemala. This region is a drainage basin about sixty miles long and twenty miles wide and is covered by tropical rain forest; the Mayas, in fact, are only one of two peoples to develop an urban culture in a tropical rainforest. The principal city in this region was Tikal, but the spread of urbanization extended south to Honduras; the southernmost Mayan city was Copan in northern Honduras. In the Guatemalan highlands to the north, Mayan culture developed less fully. The highlands are more temperate and seem to have been the main suppliers of raw materials to the central urban centers. The largest and most complete urban center was Palenque. The other major region of Mayan development was the Yucatan peninsula making up the southern and eastern portions of modern-day Mexico. This is a dry region and, although urban centers were built in this region, including Chichen Itza and Uxmal (pronounced "Oosh-mal"); most scholars believe that this was a culturally marginal area. After the abandonment of the Classic Mayan cities, the Yucatán peninsula became the principal region of a new, synthetic culture called Toltec-Mayan which was formed when Toltec's migrating from the north integrated with indigenous Maya peoples.

The Maya civilization shares many features with other Mesoamerican civilizations due to the high degree of interaction and cultural diffusion that characterized the region. Advances such as writing, epigraphy, and the calendar did not originate with the Maya; however, their civilization fully developed them. Maya influence can be detected as far as central Mexico, more than 1000 km (625 miles) from the Maya area. Many outside influences are found in Maya art and architecture, which are thought to result from trade and cultural exchange rather than direct external conquest. The Maya peoples never disappeared, neither at the time of the Classic period decline nor with the arrival of the Spanish conquistadores and the subsequent Spanish colonization of the Americas. Today, the Maya and their descendants form sizable populations throughout the Maya area and maintain a distinctive set of traditions and beliefs that are the result of the merger of pre-Columbian and post-Conquest ideologies.

Maya codices (singular codex) are folding books stemming from the pre-Columbian Maya civilization, written in Maya hieroglyphic script on Mesoamerican paper, made from the inner bark of certain trees, the main being the wild fig tree or Amate (Ficus glabrata).

Paper, generally known by the Nahuatl word amatl, was named by the Mayas huun. The folding books are the products of professional scribes working under the patronage of the Howler Monkey Gods. The Maya developed their huun-paper around the 5th century, the same era that the Romans did, but their paper was more durable and had a better writing surface than papyrus. The codices have been named for the cities in which they eventually settled. The Dresden codex is generally considered the most important of the few that survive.

One aspect of Mayan art is often overlooked, and that is the tremendous variety of excellence in style and design that it contains. Ancient Greek vase paintings are equally excellent but in comparison to the Mayan are monostylistic. Mayan art gave almost free reign to the artist, who was not required to produce a product that fit "the canon of the culture" in every way. In its encouragement of individual genius and its variations from one workshop to another, the products of which were intended in good part to be given or sold to the royalty of other cities, Mayan vase paintings are more akin to the art of the modern period than the art of any other pre-modern people. The principal valuation seems to have been on artistic quality rather than adherence to standardized forms. Furthermore, like Greek and Chinese artists, Mayan painters and sculptors sometimes signed their work. Accordingly, their work was not a "cultural product" or a "city's product" but a person's product. It appears that literacy was confined to the elite (as in all pre-modern cultures) and artists and the literate were of the same class; indeed, it is probable that Mayan artists were often the younger sons and daughters of the ahaus, the rulers, of Mayan cities.

The Maya had specific techniques to create, inscribe, paint, and design pottery. To begin creating a ceramic vessel the Maya had to locate the proper resources for clay and temper. The present-day indigenous Maya, who currently live in Guatemala, Belize and southern Mexico, still create wonderful ceramics. Prudence M. Rice provides a look at what the current Guatemalan Maya use today for clay. Highland Guatemala has a rich geological history comprised mainly from a volcanic past. The metamorphic and igneous rock, as well as the sand and ash from the pumice areas provide many types of tempering. In the area, there are a range of clays that create varied colors and strengths when fired. Today's Maya locate their clays in the exposed river systems of the highland valleys. It is hypothesized that the ancient people obtained their clay by the same method as today's Maya. The clays are located in exposed river systems of the highland valleys. Most likely, due to the climatic similarities over the last millennia it is likely that these same deposits or similar ones could have been used in early times.

Once the clay and temper were collected, pottery creation began. The maker would take the clay and mix it with the temper (the rock pieces, ash, or sand). Temper served as a strengthening device for the pottery. Once worked into a proper consistency, the shape of the piece was created.

A potter's wheel was not used in creating this pottery. Instead, they used coil and slab techniques. The coil method most likely involved the formation of clay into long coiled pieces that were wound into a vessel. The coils were then smoothed together to create walls. The slab method used square slabs of clay to create boxes or types of additions like feet or lids for vessels. Once the pot was formed into the shape, and then it would have been set to dry until it was leather hard, and then it was painted, inscribed, or slipped. The last step was the firing of the vessel.

Like the Ancient Greeks, the Maya created clay slips from a mixture of clays and minerals. The clay slips were then used to decorate the pottery. By the fourth century, a broad range of colors including yellow, purple, red, and orange were being made. However, some Mayan painters refrained from using many colors and used only black, red, and occasionally cream. This series of ceramics is termed the "Codex-style", it being similar to the style of the Pre-Columbian books.

From the 5th century AD onwards, post-firing stucco was adopted from Teotihuacan. By preparing thin quicklime, the Maya added mineral pigments that would dissolve and create rich blues and greens that added to their artistic culture. Many times this post-fire stucco technique was mixed with painting and incising. Incising is carving deeply or lightly into partially

The Elevation to Divinity

dried clay to create fine detailed designs. This technique was mostly popular during the Early Classic Period."

Beatrize showed us some rare examples they had at the Hacienda of ancient art from the Mayas and we felt blessed that we were able to behold such ancient well preserved pieces of ancient art. She said she could go on forever but realized it was getting late and she had a lot of things to prepare for her next day treatments.

We used their copy machine to copy the printed map of Kioshi and several maps of Ycatan, Mexico and the world and the map of ancient Maya reign that Beatrize had shown us. We then split these in 2 and drove back to Merida where I dropped Osiris at the corner of the street, we would both do the same things that night and that was a close study of the maps.

We had agreed that once we had an insight we would use our Mexican phones to contact each other and drive to the destination without mentioning or revealing its coordinates or whereabouts, a simple "I've got it and a time to leave" was all we needed.

It wasn't a simple task as I did not have the right tools for a task like that and I kept drawing points on maps using the picture and the map of Kioshi until I suddenly realized that I could use the computer to help me with the parameters I had in front of me, I used the image of the dagger as the front layer, through which I looked as if they were binoculars and the maps where the layers underneath which I could zoom in and out. Then the answer came to me and before I reached for my phone it already rang, it was Osiris: he said "I've got it 5 pm" I replied "me too"....

I woke up Charlotte and said that later that day we would have to go into the jungle, she said:"I have prepared for this" and went to fetch the parcel out of the locker. It were three military outfits from a military train camp. Camouflage pants and long-sleeved khaki t-shirts and three berets. She said: "I am sure they will be very useful once we are in the jungle, as there are several military bases that we might come across. I've asked Eduardo where they are and what would be the best way for us to not get caught if we were to do a night dropping just for the exciting fun of it. He said dress up as if you were one of us, hide your hair under the beret, even at the camps its full darkness at night and avoid using the car near to one of the bases as they will notice the car lights from afar. He wished us a fun night!"

I decided I would call Osiris to ask him to bring with him a flashlight, a rope and a machete. As agreed we picked him up at 5 pm at the same corner as the day before. On the way we stopped at the temple of Uxmal where we were just in time for the evening performance that was a light show where all temples would communicate with one another. I decided to record the whole play with my film camera, as it might provide us with some useful information about the region, although it was all in Spanish, it wasn't very difficult to feel what it was all about, it was all about the soul. After the play we decided to stop for a meal in Tical, where we arrived in a town that was very typical Mexican, the people didn't speak Spanish but an Ycatanese Indian. The food was very good and very fresh and ever so cheap and the service was done in silence but in a very friendly way. We were sure that we were at a safe place so we decided to put our heads together and share some of our views about the location of the hidden temple. We were only an hour away from where we thought the location to be and it was already late enough so it seemed a good idea to drive towards the jungle, we saw a few signs on the way that pointed out a military base. When we arrived near the point where we could no longer make use of the car, as the road became too narrow and overgrown by trees, we hid the car a bit further away from the road. Although we had taken our precautions we waited there for a while to see if we were followed. Luckily that was not the case. I changed my clothes and put on my military clothing. Osiris did the same and also Charlotte who had to stay with the car in case something went wrong. She could go for help as we noticed the cellphone signal had completely disappeared. We had not thought about that and we knew that the use of walky talkies could be picked up by the military base nearby as they used the same means of communication. Charlotte had been very helpful with providing us with all that inside information. We set off the two of us. From there Osiris used the machete to get through the dense forest. After a few miles we came to the temple. The temple was exactly where our calculations had said it would be. The temple was completely hidden and overgrown by trees, bushes and weeds and had sunk into a lower level, probably by an earthquake. The temple sat on a lower substructure almost 2 levels lower than the ground above it.

Just a part of the temple was still accessible, it seemed to have sunk centuries ago, it seemed strange to approach a temple from the top first and then try to find a way to climb down. I worried a bit that we might not be able to succeed in our mission this evening as we had not foreseen that the temple would be under the earth surface.

We started walking down the stairs that had remained intact and accessible from the temple top towards the base, but around what could have been the middle of the temple we could not go any further as the earth surrounded the sides completely. We decided to climb back to the top. At

The Elevation to Divinity

the top of the overgrown temple we started to remove the weeds, bushes and other plants. And finally we could see the center of the temple from its top, I assume its height must have been around 40 meters and the top was 4 meters and then it went gradually wider to its base. The temple had a weird shape, almost octagonal but there were not 8 sides but only 7. I saw that each 7 meters downwards there was a narrower piece of half a meter. I tried to picture the temple in all its grace in front of me and due to the unusual shape it was difficult to picture it in its fullness as we could not go lower and measure it more accurate, we could only guess that what we were able to see would repeat itself all the way down.

I climbed towards the center of the top and was in the middle of 7 sides of the temple at the top. I asked Osiris to throw me the measure device and found that each of the sides were 60 cm. in the middle of the lines from all the corners I drew a circle. Apart from my drawings the whole surface was empty and flat. I was confused. I looked at my bracelet and went over the signs one by one: MUAN – PAX –KAYAB – CUMHU – UAYEB – POP – OU –ZIP – ZOTZ – TZEC – XUL – YAXKIN – MOL- CHEN – YAX – ZAC – CEH – MAC – KANKIN the Maya civilization used a 365 day long year, called Haab, which had 19 months. Each of the first 18 months was 20 days long, and the names of the months were pop, no, zip, zotz, tzec, xul, yoxkin, mol, chen, yax, zac, ceh, mac, kankin, muan, pax, koyab, cumhu. Instead of having names, the days of the months were denoted by numbers starting from 0 to 19. The last month of Haab was called uayet and had 5 days denoted by numbers 0, 1, 2, 3, and 4. The Maya believed that this month was unlucky, I remember that Beatrize told me to consult this calendar incase I got lost in time and space, and that's exactly how I felt, in the middle of a riddle between geometric shapes, vectors and an ancient calendar. I started grouping the months to each of the 7 sides, and started with pop, no, zip on one side, zotz, tzec and xul on the second one, yoxkin, mol, chen on the 3rd, yax, zac and ceh on the 4th, mac, kankin, muan on the 5th, pax, koyab, cumhu on the 6th and on the 7th I placed uayet + 5x uayet. I was now in the middle of Haab. I started drawing sixty lines towards the center from each of the 6 sides that contained 3 months, then I did the same for the remaining 7th side, I drew twenty lines towards the center, lines that had more width between them than the other 6 sides. The answer had to be in the 5 days that were considered unlucky. So I started from the center moving my way up, starting my counting backwards, the 5 unlucky days drawn into the 7 segments, starting at the most northern side moving anti clockwise, using the width from the sixty lines that presented the days of 3 months. When I had finished drawing I stood up and pointed my flashlight closely to the remaining part that contained no unlucky days. I was then that I recognized the perfect triangle shape I had seen before, the same 7 edges. The dagger.

I waved the light towards Osiris who was busy trying to find a clue or a sign at the sides that were accessible. I asked him to hand me the dagger and climb up and help me find the way in. We placed the dagger with the handle of the spot but it was smaller so that was not the way in then Osiris started redrawing the lines I had drawn in chalk now with the dagger and the stone seemed to melt under the engravings of the dagger. We removed the parts that were cut away and found a hatch with a round handle. It was of course as solidly closed as possible and we had to use a big branch of one of the trees we had cut to use as a lever. Under the hatch was a deep hole I shone in this hole with the flashlight. Deep down I could detect something that looked like a surface, shiny but not wet. We threw a stone down and counted the seconds until it reached the surface. I estimated the depth to be between 40 and 50 meters.

I felt that we had to go down. Osiris and I fixed the rope which we had brought with us around the ring of the hatch which we then turned to its side blocking it by the branch of the tree. I doubted if the rope would be long enough but Osiris assured me it was exactly 50 meters long. We lowered ourselves into the temple, one at a time.

I grabbed the rope first and went down gently into the dark room. I progressed slowly and I went through layers of ancient cobwebs. When I finally reached the bottom I used the flash light. Rats and other vermin fled away. I saw that the walls were covered with hieroglyphs. I noticed that the room contained an altar at the back of the wall. I ordered Osiris to come down. He progressed slowly down the rope although there were no layers of cobwebs for him. When he was at the bottom I gave him the flashlight. The rope had been almost long enough as I had used almost 2 meters of it to fix it very tightly to the ring of the hatch. My experience in bondage proofed of good use for this. How different this adventure seemed from the life I usually lead, where I am worshipped and served and attended to my every whim. Here I had to do all the thinking and puzzling and climbing and so on, all by myself, with Osiris at my side of course, doing just as much.

Weird thoughts ran through my head at that moment when I thought about my house and my studio, worries about bills I had forgotten to pay cos of the imprisonment, the travelling, the pregnancy of Honey, the quest that had completely obsessed all my thinking. What if this was all just a

The Elevation to Divinity

fantasy of me and Osiris we had created in our own minds and influenced each other with visions and hallucinations. I started thinking back about the moment I started using mind control on Osiris, so could I actually still trust his judgment after I had brainwashed him with my own obsessions?

Still we were here at the bottom of a hidden or lost temple that no-one else had found for centuries. The inside seemed to have been untouched; I must have been very close in my estimation that it was about 50 meters deep. I started thinking how the temple was constructed as from the inside you could only see that it had 7 edges. I calculated in head that there were 6 segments of 7 meters and between each segment was a ridge of 49 cm so that was 42 meters + 2,94 meters or if there were 7 segments it would have been 49 cm + 3,43 meters so a total of 52,43 meters. I went for the last option, thinking about the length of the rope and the stretch in the rope itself. That was so typically me, trying to figure out the exact height as I needed that to help me visualize the temple as it was. The 7 edges made it look sharper than an octagonal shape would have done and although they were all of the same dimension, it gave the illusion that they were all different and the field of depth was also very much like an illusion. I couldn't wait to measure each of the 7 edges at the base to see if my eyes were really playing tricks on me … But Osiris had the flashlight and had started to study the hieroglyphs. After some time he came to a part that seemed to interest him more than other parts. He started to translate it and winked me to come and have a look; there are the hieroglyphs you burned into my skin. After Osiris had pointed them out I was able to recognize them. Osiris translated this particular piece further. "She is the righteous. She is it who reveals the light. She is the one who is in her fourth life on earth. The first three times she entered this temple as a man. The fourth time she enters as a superior female Goddess. She wards off the evil from the earth."

Osiris went with his hand over the text he had just read out loud from end to beginning when suddenly the wall on which this was written seemed to move backwards all of a sudden out of nowhere THE VOICE we had heard before in our visions started to talk. We looked at each other startled. "Yes Goddess Ira, for an expedition you have the proper clothes on, however for the coming special occasion they are not suitable. A ray of blue light flashed towards me and I found myself wearing the same clothes I wore in my hallucinations and the first brandings of Osiris. The black latex catsuit high waist cut and the thigh-high high heeled black boots. "Now you look sophisticated the voice said. For the first time in this temple you have a superior female body. Osiris this is done to cover her male traits she has acquired during her previous three lives as a male on earth. Leave these clothes here Goddess Ira. It will be a close race between good and evil. The time has to be right in accordance with the Maya calendar. Beware there are mistakes made by scholars. You have to eliminate them. Find out the exact date and time. The answer is behind the altar. Find out the places where the stone and the artifacts have to be put. When the time is right the golden amulet of Osiris can be removed without lethal consequences for Osiris. You also have to follow the exact procedures. The clues are in this room. If everything goes well a mechanism will be activated that brings you both to the divine room. If you fail you both will be swallowed by the devourer. Your hearts will be heavy from disappointment because a secret society will have succeeded and there start a blackness that will endure till the end of time. There is not much time left." Then THE VOICE faded away

We had received three directions. We had to find the right place, the right time and the right procedure. We first started to look for the right place. We thoroughly inspected the walls. We tapped the walls on all 7 sides but couldn't find any clue that could be of use for the divine mission of Goddess Ira. We inspected the floor. We swept the floor clean using leaves, especially the floor around the altar as that was made of a sort of mosaic.

Finally in the front of the altar we found a little deepening in the floor. Carefully, layer after layer, we began to remove the ancient dust and excreta of the animals. Finally we saw that it had the shape of a human body carved out in the floor of the temple. The similarity with the shape of the painting from Egypt was striking. This could not be a mistake. We had to put the stone in this place. We had to get the stone transported here and there was not a lot of time left. But what should we do with the box and the golden amulet? A riddle we could not solve.

The second direction had been the place behind the altar. Osiris knew the Maya calendar. From the hieroglyphs he understood that he had to take the religious Tzolkin calendar. He explained to me that this calendar consisted of twenty named periods of thirteen days. Each successive day, the day number plus 1. After 260 days the calendar repeats itself. But how should we calculate? I told him how I figured out the entrance to the temple by using the old calendar so it made perfect sense that a second entrance would be hidden in the other calendar. Luckily an event was described and Osiris knew when this event had taken place. It was the year 1029 after Christ. The hieroglyphs said also that we had to add the time that had elapsed since the birth of Goddess Ira. After using a calculator on the phone

The Elevation to Divinity

and taking into account the past leap years Osiris concluded that the right time would be 21 December 2012. That would be the day after tomorrow.

We also found the clues which were connected with the third direction. The ceremony should start exactly when the sun was at its peak and end exactly at midnight. When the sun was at its peak the stone should be put into the gap in front of the altar. The stone had to be 10 inches thick. The place where the two remaining items had to be placed would be revealed when the proper procedure was followed. The procedure was described in the scroll from Dewi.

After we agreed we had learned and understood what was necessary for the next step we decided to climb back up and come back the day after tomorrow with the objects. But before we climbed the rope, I ordered Osiris, to turn away his head and to close his eyes. When I started my climb I allowed Osiris to open his eyes and to hold down the rope for me to climb on. I was wearing my military clothes again. The catsuit and the boots I had left behind on the altar

Osiris used the next day to study the scroll of Dewi and me and Charlotte went to collect the stone that was sent by the inspector to one of his relatives in a town called Cholul, near Merida, when we had collected it Osiris started to cut the stone so that it was exactly 10 inches thick. Charlotte bought a few candles and incense sticks. When the day finally dawned we left early. As we were obliged to spend time in the same hotel from now on as time was no longer on our side and being careful not to be detected seemed of lesser importance than to end our mission before it was too late, we noticed that we were being watched. But Charlotte managed to call in the help of her military friends who stopped the vehicle that was following us so that way we were able to get rid of them. We drove to the hidden temple and hid the car close to where we had left it last time. We carried with us our tools, the holy objects and the candles. We walked quite a long way off-road before we withdrew into the jungle. It wasn't easy, the stone was quite heavy and large and it should not be damaged. We all carried the stone together and its was wrapped in the sheets from the bed in the hotel a woolen blanket on top of it where we had placed the other objects spread over the surface and all wrapped in another sheet. Finally we reached the temple. We had left the hatch the way we used it for our climb down, also the rope was still in position, we had just covered this up with some big banana leaves. Also this time I went first down. Once down Osiris and Charlotte pulled the rope up and tied the stone to it, using the full blanket wrapped around it and a second rope as a harness around it, Charlotte, just like her mother was an artist with ropes. With some difficulty they were able to lower the stone carefully through the hole at the top of the temple. I guided the stone the last few meters so that a soft landing was guaranteed. Then Osiris went down with the box and the candles. Charlotte would stay up the top of the temple as lookout.

In the temple I ordered Osiris to turn his head away from me and to close his eyes and I dressed myself with the clothes that were layed out for me on the altar. In the temple we arranged things and prepared ourselves for what would come. It was either to be swallowed up by the devourer or to be successful and save the world.

I asked Osiris to lie down naked on the altar and to close his eyes again. It was not allowed to open them. The scroll of Dewi prescribed a peculiar sacrifice before we could continue. Out of my bag I took a circular branding iron with a wooden handle. In the middle of the circle was written my name IRA.

Using a burner, I made the branding iron very hot. When it had the right temperature I walked to the altar and I pressed the branding iron, which had a yellow and red glow, on the front of the erect penis of Osiris. The smell of burning flesh mingled with the stale air of the temple. I had a brain orgasm and was happy with the result because the impression was clearly visible.

It is the ultimate sign that I owned for ever this man. I would decide if and how and with whom his thing would be used if we would survive. I alone have the Devine powers to link him in mind and body to one of my female associates. He belongs forever to my household. In a flesh I saw in front of me two persons. One female and one male. Both were blindfolded, gagged and their hands were tied. They don't know each other. I was saying aloud the vows and duties and they nodded there assent.

When Osiris had recovered a bit we tried to put the stone in place in the space in front of the altar. It was a perfect match. The sun shone precisely through the middle of the hole at the top of the temple, we knew it was time. Although the Ego of Osiris matched my Ego as closely as possible and words were no longer necessary I nevertheless asked Osiris if he was ready. He nodded. He was well aware of the fact that the last tiny part of his Ego would die here. The gurus call this experiencing the big death. I then ordered Osiris to lie down on the stone. I arranged him so that his figure matched precisely the outline of it. The outline of the stone which coincided with the outline of the daughter of Maat. The sunbeam fell precisely on the golden amulet Osiris wore around his neck. It reflected to a place on the altar. Without hesitation, I removed the amulet from the neck of Osiris and walked towards the altar. There was an irresistible force that pulled my hand and the amulet towards the altar. The force became so strong that it tore the amulet out of my hand and it snapped on the carved out image of the sun on the altar. I heard a noise behind me where Osiris was. Osiris cried out. It was as though the temple, even the world around him collapsed and all were absorbed into the abyss of the absolute. I turned around and ran back to Osiris to hear him exhale his last breath. Osiris was dead. I was shocked and filled with grief although I knew that this was in accordance with the ancient text and that death was just another way of being, another consistence or coherence.

The following hours I felt abandoned and utterly alone but I could not afford the feeling of sadness or grief, I had to carry on and perform and finalize my mission. I placed the candles around the death body of Osiris. I had learned to understand the power of the words and it was my role to let the deceased body of Osiris rise into the god Osiris, to be reborn later. To attain re-birth, Osiris had to pass a number of rituals and test. I washed his corpse renewing his life through ritual washing with sacred water. I wrapped the body, except the penis and balls, of Osiris in linen bandages. With a special silver knife I removed his penis and balls from his body. In accordance with the instructions I had to do this because the body of women consists of fourteen parts and my soul had to descend into the body of Osiris. Where his marked erect penis and balls had been a few moment earlier I made an incision at the place where women have their slit. This created hole I then closed with a needle and threat. The dead Osiris was not only castrated but had received in his afterlife a pussy.

Some of the bandages were inscribed with spells and prayers which I had found in the scroll from Dewi. Once he was wrapped I performed various rituals including reciting prayers, sprinkling water, lighting incense. The exact procedure was written in the scroll from Dewi, if you used the right code. During these long hours I sometimes doubted if I had used the right code.

Almost at midnight I drank the drink made in accordance with the recipe I had found in the scroll from Dewi. I then unrolled the body of Osiris. This was not a very easy task especially the opening of his mouth was problematic. But also this had to be done. The only part that was not problematic was his penis which I also had wrapped in linen bandages and had put on his corpse where it once had been attached to his body. His penis with the clearly visible tattoo was limb since the penis has no muscle tissue. It was now midnight. It was a period that the New Moon and the sun occupy the same part in the sky. It was the time of the union of these two energies. It was the seed-time, the time for a new beginning. It was only now, at this moment, that it would be possible to open the box. In the box there was a silver moon. I put the silver moon around the neck of Osiris. The light of the moon reflected on this amulet. I followed the reflection with my eyes. The light stopped at the front of the altar next to the sun amulet. I took the moon amulet from Osiris and went to the altar. Although the force was not as strong as the force I had experienced earlier that day with the sun amulet, the force was strong enough to guide my hand to the altar to a place it alongside the sun amulet where the reflection had show me to place it. I put the moon there and again I heard the click when it fixed itself at the altar. The symbols of what was and what will be were now in place next to each other on the altar.

At exactly midnight I stood over Osiris and I peed over the whole body with my large waterfall of what seemed like pure gold I had held inside for more than 12 hours. When the pressure became less strong I stood alongside the ears of Osiris and emptied myself completely into his mouth. Something strange happened with the stone. I lost my balance and fell onto the ice-cold body of Osiris. The stone pulverized and we fell into a lower level, when I looked around it seemed we had fallen into a sarcophagus. Before I could climb out, the lid of the sarcophagus closed itself and I was casted in with the body of Osiris. The body of Osiris opened up and surrounded my body. Osiris had become my sarcophagus it was obvious that he was the chosen one who had sacrificed his mortal being to provide me access to my divine status. However it was pitch dark and I could hardly move. I felt I was inside the icy corpse of Osiris. My clothes had dissolved and I found myself completely naked. I panicked a little but I forced myself to stay calm. I felt that my Egyptian soul, which I had created inside Osiris, did interflow with me. Suddenly I became aware of a hard object that lay beneath the center of mine or Osiris forehead. With great difficulty I was able to move my hand under my forehead and reached for the object I could clearly feel under my head and the split head of Osiris. It was a ring. I put the ring on my ring finger. The sarcophagus opened. A very bright light lit up the room and I saw myself laying, a bit dazed and confused, in the body of Osiris THE VOICE came back out of nowhere and spoke: "Goddess Ira you have accomplished your quest. You are purified, cleaned and without sin like Adam and Eve were before they ate the apple. You know no shame. You have proven that you are the Goddess with the seven special qualities.

The Elevation to Divinity

From now on you always have to wear this ring. It will ward off the evil from the earth and it gives you the power to decide which supreme females can become Goddesses and who will be your chosen servants."

"Through you the chosen six Goddesses will experience mental enlightenment in advance of others and be recognized as the new leaders of the world. Through you and the chosen Goddesses you will take control of the Earth and its destiny. You the seven Goddesses will enlighten humanity. The Goddesses will teach human mankind that they can make a choice between good and evil. Without evil there is no good! Each soul has the opportunity to make those choices very often in his life. The souls spiritual development can be compared to a three which many branches. When one comes to the fork one has two choices. An evil one and a good one but one can only choose one direction. The result of moving along these trajectories will be that some of the souls will become the abode of the Creator and others will become the abode of destruction. It is thanks to you that the new leaders of humanity will break free of centuries of false doctrines, destructive indoctrinations and absurd ideas. The destiny of humankind is the revelation of truth and the expansion of consciousness. This period is destined to free their minds of ignorance and delusion forever. You the Goddesses will integrate and unify human mankind with the energy of the universe. Once enlightened each human being will begin his or her individual journey within, and strive to reach his full spiritual potential. There will be no more derision but spiritual living. The mind will be liberated. Through you and the other Goddesses human mankind will develop friendship in a more elevated sense. Love and friendship will have nothing more to do with possessing or ego. The idea of love as a possession ends. There will be an era of peace, of unity and of love. The individuality will integrate with the unity of humanity. Through you and the other Goddesses humanity will break free from the past and invent the future they desire in their society and in their person. Humanity will not any longer destroy the earth but will preserve the earth and the universe. All institutions as you know them will adapt in time to this new reality. The corrupt foundations of society start to crumble from now on."

I went out of the body of Osiris and the sarcophagus. Osiris would be the first chosen one. I removed the stitches from the created pussy. Then I took a golden needle and golden thread which I had found on a satin pillow on the altar and I started to sew his penis to his dead body, also here my skills of my medical fetish proved to be very useful again. When I had finished sewing and checked my work, I touched with my ringed finger certain body parts of Osiris, his ears, his nose, his mouth, his eyes and his recently marked penis. My soul left through the ring and entered his lifeless body. A strange swirl movement of mist moved inside his body and when this calmed down, he opened his eyes, moved his hands as if it was the first time he ever used them or was aware of them.

Osiris had regained life, he was reborn, pure, unstained, without knowledge and without sin. Like Adam before him he knew no shame. For the first time he could see me completely, me naked but it no longer mattered as he looked at me with innocent eyes. He was the man who had given up his Ego and his mortal being for me to make it possible for me to interflow into his body.

Without false modesty I know that I look great. I have not only a beautiful face and great legs but I also have beautiful breasts size C85. Osiris later told me he did found them very, very attractive. My breasts size makes my hips look even tinier with my size xs. I know that not only Osiris but most men find this an irresistible combination. He admired the large tattooed dragon on my left side of my back which starts at my left shoulder and ends at my waist. Anyway, my appearance was identical with the appearance of the daughter of Maat which had been depicted on the stone. I noticed that Osiris was still very cold and I warmed him with my body by holding him like a new born oversized baby.

The circle was completed. My mission was accomplished. I am the righteous and had to lead the six other supreme women to the Goddess state and six other chosen ones to serve us into the way towards the light. Osiris was reborn and had a new identity. He was again a man connected in eternal love with me his Goddess Ira. That's why the brandings and tattoos made by me are still on his body.

Follow your way my friend. Sometimes the road is long but sometimes the road is short. Who knows? Nobody. The essence is that you never know exactly where you are going and when you come to the end. The inimitable life manifest itself full of new and rich events and endless possibilities. The only thing you can do is follow your heart, seize the opportunities and put consistent energy in them. That is the way I Goddess Ira live. That's the way Osiris soul, mind and body became mine. That's the way Osiris ego went up into my ego. From the outside he is still Osiris but from the inside he is me. The only thing that changed in his appearance is the color of his eyes; they have taken on the color of my very specific green eyes.

The circle of his brands is the sign of our eternal covenant which cannot be broken. True freedom lies in the human mind. It is the freedom to be who we really are. Osiris used his freedom of mind and decided that I make the decisions in the future for him. I used my freedom of mind to accept his wish. His future will coincide with my future. The snakes of the caduceaus in the pubis of Osiris represent both of us.

About the Author

Goddess Ira has many years of experience as an international dominatrix and Osiris has an in-depth knowledge about ancient history.

Goddess Ira is an artist, performer and creator and studied at the academie van schone kunsten in Antwerp (Belgium).Goddess Ira has one daughter. Osiris studied history and was a teacher in history. He has two children. Both have a profound interest in the spiritual world. This common interest led to the introduction of Osiris in the BDSM world. Eventually she became his soul mate and he received from her his collar.

It was at a kitchen table in Belgium, were Goddess Ira lives, that the idée arose to write a book together. It was fun to blend our knowledge and experiences together in this book. We learned a lot from each other and from the consulted sources. We learned that the souls spiritual development can be compared to a three which many branches. When one comes to the fork one has two choices. An evil one and a good one but one can only choose one direction.

We think that the destiny of humankind is the revelation of truth and the expansion of consciousness and hope that some of the contents of this book will promote the development of friendship in a more elevated sense. Love and friendship should in our view have nothing to do with possessing or ego. We hope that our book will contribute to a better understanding and a better world.